I0785031

Hounded By Murder

By Ellen Fannon

ISBN-13:978-1-968792-57-2

<u>ALSO BY ELLEN FANNON</u>

Other People's Children
Save the Date – 2022 Christian Indie Award winner
Don't Bite the Doctor
Honor Thy Father – Episode One
Honor Thy Father —Episode Two
Dogged by Murder

<u>LOVE IN THE WIND SERIES</u>

Love in the Wind —Book One —2024 Living Water Award Winner
Falling For a Cowboy – Book Two
Loves' Trail of Redemption —Book Three

Chapter One

"You're late!"

I froze mid-step, one foot still on the welcome mat of the Dalton County Animal Shelter, where I volunteered my veterinary services one day a week. My arms were full with my medical bag slung over my shoulder, a travel mug of lukewarm coffee in one hand, and a packet of dog biscuits in the other.

"Excuse me?" I turned toward the voice. A bleached blonde with an inch of dark roots glared at me, her arms crossed over her chest. Her red nails, long enough to double as switchblades, drummed against her elbows. After a month away on a mission trip to Belize, I had been out of circulation and had no idea who this woman was.

I blinked. "I'm sorry, but I don't know you. I'm Dr. Amanda Reynolds." I smiled, transferred the dog treats to my hand with the coffee, and stuck out my free hand. "I volunteer here once a week."

The blonde ignored my outstretched hand. "I *know* who you are. And you're late. I'm Ms. Dilly, the new director, and I don't care if you're a volunteer or not. I expect you to be on time."

New director? My brain did a stutter step. "Where's Frances?" I loved the older, jovial lady who had run this shelter for decades. I'd had no inkling she was planning on leaving.

"Frances quit and moved to Georgia or Tennessee or somewhere." Ms. Dilly flipped her hand like it didn't really matter. "Thank goodness. She left this place in a mess. This shelter needs a firm hand."

Too stunned to respond, I bristled under the words. Frances had the kindest heart of anyone I had ever met, and she ran the shelter efficiently and with a warmth that made everyone, human or animal, feel instantly at home. Everybody liked her. Frances didn't just run the shelter— she *was* the shelter.

"You have work piled up from your absence. I suggest you get to it." Ms. Dilly pivoted and marched back into the office.

I drifted into the veterinary suite in a daze. Vanessa, the technician, was drawing up sedatives for surgery patients.

"Van, what's going on around here? What happened to Frances?"

Vanessa crossed the length of the small room and grabbed my arm. "I'm so glad you're back. You won't believe what's been going on." She shot a furtive glance at the door as though eavesdroppers hovered just outside. Maybe they did, because she even took a peek out into the hall before continuing.

"Frances slipped on a wet kennel floor right after you left and broke her hip. Her daughter insisted this job was too much for her to continue at her age and urged her to quit and move to North Carolina so she could care for her."

My chest tightened. Poor Frances. I hadn't even gotten the chance to say goodbye.

I rubbed my temples, which had started to throb. "So where did this . . . Ms. Dilly person, the charm school dropout, come from?"

"I see you've met Margot, our new director." Vanessa rolled her eyes and blew out a breath that stirred the bangs on her forehead. "That's a mystery nobody can figure out. County Commissioner Stanley Quackenbush appointed her."

It figured. Stanley Quackenbush had the judgment of a man who'd order sushi at a Mexican restaurant.

Vanessa looked around again and lowered her voice in a conspiratorial whisper. "A few of us think there's something fishy about her appointment. Something *very* fishy."

My head swam. After four weeks in the jungle, I had been looking forward to returning to my small bit of charity work at home. I'd always felt it my civic duty to give back to the community where I could, and working at the animal shelter provided a much-needed service. I'd enjoyed caring for the hundreds of animals who had the misfortune to come through our doors and always loved the happy endings when they found their forever homes. The staff had been wonderful to work with, and the days I spent here helped me decompress from the daily pressures of working in a busy, demanding practice.

"Gary is fit to be tied," Vanessa added. "If anyone should have been given the director's position, it's him."

Gary, Frances' second-in-command, who took over when she was unavailable, had been with the shelter for almost ten years and knew all the ins and outs.

"So, what's Gary doing now?"

Vanessa flattened her lips. "He's trying to do his job, like he's always done, but the dragon-lady has him on a short leash. Talk about a micromanager."

"Is Margot always this unpleasant?" I asked. "She jumped down my throat the minute I walked through the door because I was—" I consulted my watch—"ten minutes late." As if I punched the clock as a volunteer.

"You have no idea." Vanessa shook her head, her frizzy black curls taking on a life of their own. "She's made this place a living nightmare. Most of us are thinking about jumping ship and finding other jobs."

My heart clenched. I hated losing the people I enjoyed working with. And, if push came to shove, I might have to jump ship with them. This job didn't pay enough (hah!) to warrant being brow-beaten by a bullying director.

As if my thoughts had conjured up the horrible woman, Margot burst through the door. "Why haven't you got the surgeries started?" she demanded, fisted hands on her hips.

Vanessa startled and dropped the syringe she was holding. The uncapped needle flew like a trajectory through the air, landing just short of Margot's pristine, white Versace sneakers. She leaped back with a screech worthy of a horror film.

"This is unacceptable!" she barked. "Do you have *no* training in safety protocol?"

"Sorry, Ms. Dilly," Vanessa muttered, bending to retrieve the syringe.

Margot turned her hawk eyes on me. "We have ten animals waiting to be spayed or neutered so they can be adopted out. I want those done by noon."

Anger crawled up my throat. Squaring my shoulders, I said, "Now just a minute, Margot—"

"*Ms.* Dilly," she corrected.

I arched an eyebrow. "I am the veterinarian in charge of veterinary services here. The surgeries will take as long as they take. I will not rush. Especially for some arbitrary timeline."

Her nostrils flared. "In case you haven't noticed, *Dr.* Reynolds, we have other animals waiting for intake exams, lab testing, and treatments." She wrinkled her nose in a derisive sneer. "Oh, that's right. You wouldn't know what's on the schedule because *you were late.*"

I took a deep breath through my nose and slowly counted to five. "Everything that needs to be done will be done," I said through gritted teeth. Schedule indeed! I had never worked a schedule at the shelter in three years. I simply stayed until I'd completed all the work. Some days took longer than others.

"And I'm the person who needs to assure everything gets done. Lest you assume otherwise, *I am* the one in charge around here. My shelter. My rules."

We locked eyes in a stare-down until Vanessa cleared her throat, causing both our gazes to drift to her. "I'm ready to sedate the first patient."

"I'm coming," I said, giving a pointed look to Margot, hoping she'd take the hint and leave.

I followed Vanessa into the holding room to the first cage, where a handsome orange tabby cat waited. "Margot needs to go back to her office and shuffle papers," I grumbled.

Vanessa snorted. "Told you." She pulled the cat from his cage and restrained him while I injected the sedative. He let out an unholy yowl and hissed. Vanessa set him back in the cage, where he sat in a sulky heap and glared at us.

"Sorry, dude." I let out a sigh and nodded toward the door. "Van, go see if she's gone."

"Why me? I've had to put up with her every day for the past three weeks. You've only had the pleasure for a few minutes."

Vanessa had me there. I stepped to the door and peeked around the corner. Good. No Margot.

"The coast is clear."

We went back into the veterinary suite and began laying out the instruments for the cat neuter. "Unless that woman and I can come to an understanding about each other's boundaries, I'm not sure I can continue working here," I said, regret washing over me. I didn't want to leave. I liked the shelter.

Vanessa groaned. "Oh, please don't leave. I nearly lost my mind while you were gone. That woman had me doing everything but technician work."

I frowned. "But you said everyone was thinking about quitting."

She bit her lip. "Yeah, but where else would I go? Nobody's hiring."

So, Vanessa had already done some looking around.

"I'll talk to her later. Maybe we just got off on the wrong foot. Each of us staking out our territories. Let's forget about her for now and neuter a cat. That will make both of us feel better."

The morning buzzed along as we worked through the surgery roster. Once I was in my zone, I nearly blocked out the way the morning had started with Margot Dilly breathing down my neck. Nearly. Something still nagged at me, like a fly circling just outside swatting range.

It hit me on the next-to-last patient—a female Great Dane. A dog roughly the size of a Smart Car squeezed onto my surgical table.

"Van," I said, as I delved elbow deep into the belly of the behemoth, "have you noticed anything odd about today's surgery lineup?"

"Besides the fact that you need a bigger table?"

"Besides that." I poked through loops of intestine with all the care of a woman searching for her keys in a massive purse. "Every patient today, except the cranky orange cat, has been a purebred."

Her brows shot up. "Now that you mention it, yeah. In fact, the kennels look like we've been taken over by the Westminster Dog Show."

I frowned behind my mask. "Shelters don't usually have this many purebreds. Not unless somebody dumped an entire breeder's stock."

Vanessa shrugged. "Beats me."

Our conversation was cut short by the grand entrance of Margot. She pursed her lips.

"It's a quarter to twelve," she announced like she'd just been appointed Time Czar of Dalton County.

A dozen sarcastic responses bounced around my skull, but my inner editor stopped them before they made it to my mouth. Probably for the best.

Her taloned hands rested on her hips again. "Are you almost finished?"

Releasing a sigh that inflated my surgical mask, I replied, "I am just starting the spay on this Great Dane, which is a bugger of a surgery, I might add. And when I'm done, I'm going to do a gastropexy on her before I close."

Margot's forehead wrinkled. Good. She didn't know what a gastropexy was. One small victory for me. Fortunately, she couldn't see my smirk of satisfaction.

"Which is?" she prodded.

"A preventive procedure to tack the stomach to the abdominal wall so she doesn't suffer a bloat or a twisted stomach later. It's standard procedure when doing an elective surgery on a big-breed dog."

"No." She shook her head emphatically. "That's an unauthorized procedure, and you're behind schedule as it is."

I stopped in mid-ovarian ligament ligation. "Margot . . . Ms. Dilly, fifteen extra minutes could save this dog's life later."

Margot's jaw clenched so hard I feared it might shatter. "I said no. You are paid to perform necessary surgeries only."

This was too much. A laugh exploded from me, sharp and ugly. "Margot, I am a *volunteer*. A volunteer who will not compromise patient care for your arbitrary rules."

I could have sworn I saw steam billow from her ears. With a dramatic spin, she stomped out—only to whirl back before the door shut.

"Mrs. Meece will be here at one. I expect you to be done by then."

Ah. Mrs. Meece. The matron saint of the Dalton County Animal Shelter. A well-intentioned, generous—albeit somewhat naïve—young woman with too much time and money on her hands. Nevertheless, her donations went a long way toward keeping the doors open and the lights on. She had apparently married "up" to an older, well-to-do gentleman who was looking for a younger, trophy wife.

Even though Marilee Meece looked like she had just stepped off the cover page of a fashion magazine and could be a bit tedious at times, I couldn't dislike the lady. But just why I had to be finished with surgery before her visit puzzled me. In the past, Frances had mainly taken on the responsibility of catering to our benefactress's whims. I usually only interacted with her in passing.

Vanessa leaned in and whispered, "Rumor has it that Mrs. Meece is not overly pleased with Frances' replacement."

"Oh?"

"I wonder why she's coming today. She was just here last week, and you know she generally comes on the first Wednesday of the month."

"Well, if I finish up by one, maybe we'll find out." I bent back to the Dane's abdomen, but before I could isolate the second ovary, Gary entered. Boy, the surgery suite was like Grand Central Station today. Never mind that the general flow of traffic into and out of a sterile environment was counterproductive.

"Remind me to post a *No Entry* sign," I muttered.

Gary stormed in, his face red enough to match his mop of hair. "I swear I'm going to *kill* that bossy broad!" His chest heaved like he'd run a marathon as he leaned against the closed door.

"It's nice to see you again, too, Gary," I said. "Since it's been four weeks."

"Sorry, Amanda. I am glad to see you. It's just that . . . Well, I guess you've discovered the change around here."

"Boy, has she," Vanessa answered for me. "Margot's been in here this morning, telling us to hurry up."

Gary's fists tightened. "If she tells me one more time . . ." He left the end of the sentence dangling, but the throbbing vein in his temple said plenty.

"I don't understand why Margot, a complete outsider, got this job instead of you," I said. "You're the logical choice." Although Gary wasn't as cuddly as Frances, he did a good job.

"That makes two of us," he said. "And I intend to go to the council meeting next week and find out why." He ran his hand through his unruly mop of carrot-colored hair. "From what I've heard, Commissioner Quackenbush made the decision to hire Margot unilaterally, without any input from the other commissioners." He pulled out a stool and parked in it, making himself at home.

"Hmm. Are they related in some way?" My idea had merit. Nepotism ran rampant in small towns.

Gary shook his head. "Not that I know of."

"Maybe they're—" A blush crept up Vanessa's cheeks. "You know."

I nearly dropped a clamp. "His mistress?" I gagged a little. "Ugh. Have you seen Stanley Quackenbush?" The image of the short, pudgy, pig-eyed man with a bad combover seared onto the back of my eyeballs, making me shudder.

Gary cocked his head. "You might be on to something, Van. I've heard Stanley thinks he's quite the ladies' man."

"Stanley Quackenbush?" I repeated. "Again, just ugh."

"Maybe someone needs to put a little bug in Mrs. Quackenbush's ear," said Vanessa.

"Not me," I said. Myrtle Quackenbush was a formidable woman who could take a bear down with one glare. I finished tying off the uterine vessels and double-ligated the uterine body. Satisfied that there was no bleeding, I worked my way north, under the massive rib cage, to find the stomach.

"You know Margot is now making us participate in monthly fund-raisers," said Gary.

"What do you mean she's *making* you?" I asked, tugging the stomach into the surgical field. Frances' fund-raisers had been optional, fun, and usually involved food. With Margot, I envisioned shackles and a cattle prod.

"Yeah," said Vanessa. "Last month, it was a golf tournament. We spent our entire day off chasing tiny white balls in the blazing sun. This month, she wants us to solicit donations from local businesses to auction off."

"I don't know about you two," said Gary, "but I'm not shlepping around town begging for handouts. Most of the local businesses are having trouble meeting their overhead as is."

"Pull that abdominal wall back, Van. That's good. Hold it just like that." She retracted the lateral wall, and I made parallel incisions in the stomach and the right abdominal wall. "I'm with you, Gary. There's no way I'm going door-to-door asking for freebies." I picked up my needle holders and grabbed the swedged-on suture, placing the needle firmly in the jaws of the needle holder.

"Next thing you know, she'll have us competing with Girl Scouts for cookie sales," grumbled Vanessa.

"I'd be willing to sacrifice eating an entire sleeve of Thin Mints if it meant I didn't have to grovel for gift certificates," said Gary.

"How much money did the golf tournament raise?" I asked.

"Beats me," said Gary. "She never showed me the receipts."

I stopped mid-suture and glanced up. "Wait. Aren't you the financial manager?"

"Not anymore. That's just one of the many duties Margot has relieved me of."

His statement caught me off guard. Gary had managed the books ever since I'd been here, and his figures were always meticulous, down to the last kibble. If Margot had pried that duty away, something reeked, and it wasn't the dirty kennel runs.

"She's also switching all our vendors," he said.

"Why? Frances always got the best deals."

"Yeah. Frances could charm discounts out of a vending machine." Nostalgia softened his expression. "Man, I miss her."

"So, what does Margot have you doing instead of financials?" I tied off the last suture and snipped the end.

He huffed out a mirthless laugh. "Well, today, I'm cleaning out the kitchen cabinets. Yesterday, cross-referencing every pet license renewal from last year and calling delinquent owners to see if Fido is still alive."

"Seriously? That sounds like a high school volunteer job." I laid my instruments down and stretched my aching back. "I'm finally ready to close now."

"Exactly. But try telling that to the harpy." He stood and shoved the stool under the desk with a screech that set my teeth on edge. "I'd better get back to scrubbing shelves before she comes looking for me. But if she steps into that kitchen one more time, someone will have to peel my hands off her neck."

I quickly sutured the abdominal wall and the skin, then glanced at the clock. Almost one. "Let's break for lunch before I pass out. We'll tackle the last surgery after."

"Sounds good to me." Vanessa gloved out and began cleaning up the surgery suite, which looked as though a cyclone had hit it. "Hope Margot doesn't parade Mrs. Meece through here."

I shrugged. "It will just prove how busy we are. Nothing says 'worthy cause' like blood spatters and a sink overflowing with surgical instruments."

Chapter Two

Fifteen minutes later, with Vanessa recovering the Dane, I stepped out of surgery and made a detour through the lobby, which led to the kennel.

"My shelter, my rules!" The words stopped me in my tracks. I looked over my shoulder to see Merlin, the African Gray parrot and official greeter for the shelter, holding court from his perch next to the filing cabinet. "My shelter, my rules," he repeated.

Dory, the volunteer receptionist, appeared unfazed as she kept her eyes glued to her computer screen.

"Uh, Dory? What happened to Merlin's usual greeting of 'Welcome to Dalton County Animal Shelter'?"

Dory glanced up. "It's amazing how quickly he picks up new phrases. But, then again, he's heard Ms. Dilly repeating those words continuously for the past three weeks."

My jaw dropped. Even the *bird* was mimicking Margot's nastiness?

"Merlin, sweetheart," I said, moving behind the desk and scratching his head. "Say, 'Welcome to Dalton County Animal Shelter.' Come on, you can do it. 'Welcome to Dalton County Animal Shelter.'"

Merlin eyed me for a moment. "*My* shelter, *my* rules!" he squawked emphatically.

I sighed and moved toward the kennel. But before I could get to the door, Marilee Meece came charging through the front door. Under one arm, she clutched a scruffy mop of a dog that looked like it had crawled out of a storm drain.

Dory sang out, "Mrs. Meece! How lovely to see you."

Lovely wasn't the word. The woman was upholstered in pink silk—at least I thought it was silk— and matching heels, with a floppy hat that kept smacking her in the face. With her free hand, she shoved the hat back onto her lacquered, blonde locks without displacing a single hair. But the Prada bag slung over her shoulder slid down her arm and whacked the filthy dog in the head, earning her a glare that suggested he might file a complaint. The matted mutt dangling under her arm clashed with her outfit worse than flip-flops at a funeral.

"Hello, Doris," she said, her voice bereft of warmth. "I want to see Ms. Dilly. Now!"

Thunderclouds gathered around Mrs. Meece's normally mild-mannered face.

Dory didn't bother to correct the woman's incorrect use of her name. "Of course. Come on back."

Curiosity yanked me along like a non-retractable leash.

They stopped outside Margot's open door, and Dory rapped lightly. "Mrs. Meece is here," she announced, unnecessarily, because without waiting for an invitation, the woman barged right in.

Margot rose and plastered what she must have considered a smile on her stern face, but it looked more like a grimace. "How nice to see you again so soon."

"Never mind that. I have a bone to pick with you." Mrs. Meece plopped into the chair across from the desk, placing the sorry-looking dog on her pristine lap as if it were a designer clutch.

"Oh?" Margot tilted her head, looking the very picture of innocence.

"Yes!" Marilee snapped. "Why did you turn this precious animal away from the shelter?"

Margot's eyes drifted to the pooch in Mrs. Meece's lap as though it'd just appeared out of thin air. "Why, I don't know what you mean."

Margot ignored me as I edged my way into the room to get a good look at our sponsor's face, which, although composed, appeared to have a storm simmering just below the surface. Her mask of calm stretched too thin to last.

"My hairdresser, Harriet, found this unfortunate little dog running the streets and brought him to you last Friday. You told her you had no room and to take him to the kill shelter downtown."

Margot's blood-red nails tapped against her chin while her eyes searched for an answer on the ceiling. "Really. That's strange. Perhaps it was one of our volunteers. I don't recall—"

"It was you." Mrs. Meece's sharp eyes shot a laser beam into Margot's. "Harriet described you to a T."

"Hmm." Margot chuffed out a laugh that didn't fool anybody. "Well, we were pretty full last week and maybe—"

"That's pure poppycock. I was here just last Wednesday, and the kennel was only half full. What are you trying to pull?" She jabbed the air with a thin, bejeweled index finger.

Margot's syrupy smile wobbled. "Why, nothing, Mrs. Meece. Marilee. May I call you Marilee?" Without waiting for permission, Margot continued. "You know I only want what's best for the animals."

"Hmph. That remains to be seen. I expect you to take this poor creature immediately and tend to his needs."

"Of course, Mrs. Meece." Margot's eyes landed on me for the first time. "Dr. Reynolds, would you be so kind as to admit this dog?" She shot me a dazzling smile, revealing a crooked front tooth.

"Certainly, Ms. Dilly," I said, scooping up the grimy pooch.

Marilee relinquished the filthy dog and smiled, apparently not noticing the dirty smudges on her silk pantsuit. "Thank you, Dr. Reynolds. I know he will be in good hands under your care."

I turned to go, but Mrs. Meece wasn't finished laying into Margot, and my feet became glued to the floor.

"And *what,* may I ask, happened to the plaque in the lobby with my husband's and my names?"

Ooh. The Meeces had a large plaque hanging right over the front desk, extolling the shelter's appreciation for their many generous contributions over the years, where all could see. My ears wiggled in eager anticipation of Margot's answer.

"Why, I have no idea, Mrs. Meece. We've been doing some cleaning and remodeling, and I'm sure it's just been misplaced." Margot rose, as though to signal the end of their meeting, but Marilee remained firmly planted in her chair, one long leg crossed over the other. Her foot jiggled with what appeared to be pent-up wrath.

"See that it's found." With her lap free, Mrs. Meece hauled her purse onto her lap and opened it, pulling out a check. "I was going to leave this with you, but I'm having second thoughts. I don't mind telling you, I don't like the way things have changed since you've taken over." She studied the check at arm's length, then frowned and tucked it back into her pocketbook.

A nervous-sounding titter escaped Margot's lips, and her face paled at the sight of the retreating money. "Please give us a chance, Mrs. Meece . . . Marilee." The second attempt to test the waters and bond with our benefactress on a first-name basis fell short, as Marilee Meece narrowed her eyes. Margot hurried on. "With any change in administration, there are growing pains. But I'm sure you'll find that the Dalton County Animal Shelter will continue to meet your high expectations."

"In the future, I'm going to insist on some stipulations in exchange for my donations. For starters, I want a key to this facility and unlimited access to any area in the shelter."

Margot's façade crumbled slightly. "I'm afraid I'm not authorized to grant that request—"

"Second, I want an accounting for every dollar I give. Third, you will use my nephew's catering service for all future events."

The smile slipped from Margot's face. "Mrs. Meece, while we appreciate your donations, I can't agree to—"

"And I want to be in charge of all events. I also want to hold a doggy fashion show this fall. Plus, I insist that the adoption fees be lowered so more animals can be moved through the shelter into their forever homes."

Margot's lips settled into a thin line, and her tone turned icy. "Impossible. I am the director, and I organize the events. And as far as adoption fees, when you consider the cost of food, veterinary care, and overhead, we're already losing money on every animal that walks out the door."

Mrs. Meece went on as though Margot hadn't spoken. "And finally, I want to be put on the board of directors and made chairperson."

Margot's palms slammed into the desk, sending several pens over the edge and tipping over her coffee mug that spilled dark liquid all over her beautifully organized blotter.

Marilee looked like she'd just been hit with a wet kennel mop.

"Now look here, you stupid, clueless bimbo!" Margot exploded. "If you think you can come in here and tell me how to run my shelter, you can think again. I don't care how much money you donate. I'm not pandering to your ridiculous conditions or allowing you to yank strings you attach to your money."

The blood drained from Mrs. Meece's face. Doubtless, no one had ever spoken to her in this manner before. "*What* did you call me?"

Margot leaned across the desk, her face contorted in anger. "A stupid, clueless bimbo!"

Marilee sucked in a huge breath and rose to her feet. "How dare you! How *dare* you!" She stabbed that index finger in Margot's direction once again. "You'll be sorry." She moved past me in a furious fog.

I should have taken my cue and followed her out, but I stood glued to the spot, unable to move. Unfortunately.

Margot directed her blazing eyes at me. "Why are you standing there? Do something with that mangy mutt!"

I hightailed it out of Margot's office and ducked into the kennel, where the smell of wet dog and bleach hit my sinuses and made me blink back tears. I wrangled our new ragamuffin resident into an empty run, latched the door, and turned to go back to surgery.

That's when a voice right behind me made me jump like I'd been tased.

"Would you like me to get some food and water for that dog?"

I whirled and almost dropped my stethoscope when I found myself staring into the face of a man who looked just like Robert Redford. Well, at least if Robert Redford were sixty years younger. And still alive. I tried to corral my galloping heartbeat, which had taken off on its own, and somehow managed to close my gaping mouth.

He shot me a dazzling, toothpaste-commercial smile of perfectly straight, blinding-white teeth, and extended a hand.

"Sorry to startle you. I'm Kip Gallagher. I just started volunteering here a couple weeks ago."

I took his hand, which was warm, strong, and unfortunately attached to a man who was about to discover that I sweat like a sinner in church when I'm nervous.

"I'm Dr. Amanda Reynolds, but please call me Amanda," I said, a little too breathlessly. "I'm the shelter veterinarian. I haven't been here for a few weeks, though, because I was on a mission trip in Belize, where our team helped build a school for one of the villages. It was a great trip, but it was really hot. And humid. And I got a bad sunburn. And the bugs! Thank goodness for Deet."

I finally reined in my tongue when my brain broke in to tell me I was babbling, and before I told him I was single. And available. But my hand was still latched onto his like I was trying to keep him from floating away.

He glanced down at our joined hands with an amused expression, and I suddenly snatched mine back so fast I thought I sprained something. Heat crept up my neck.

"Sorry," I mumbled. "It's been a weird day. First day back and all, ten surgeries, new director . . ."

His lips quirked. "Yes. She seems rather intense."

So were his eyes, and they were making it difficult to remember how to breathe. I gulped against a dry throat and looked away. "Well, I've got a surgery to finish, so I'd better go." My feet, however, didn't get the memo and stayed put, as if they were anchored in concrete.

He nodded. "Okay. Like I said, I'll get this little guy settled in."

"Thank you. It was nice meeting you." *Still not moving, Amanda. Move!*

"You, too. I guess I'll see you around." He spun away and headed to the back room, where the food was stored. I watched his broad shoulders disappear around the corner.

I stumbled back into surgery on rubbery legs, practically crashing into Vanessa, who was busy typing notes into the computer.

"Van!" I cried, clutching the counter for stability. "Why didn't you tell me about that new, hunky kennel volunteer?"

She stopped typing and gave me a stern look. "Amanda, trust me, you don't want to get mixed up with him."

"What? Why not?"

"Because," she said, pausing dramatically, "he's here doing community service hours as part of his parole conditions."

Chapter Three

Boy, talk about someone dumping a bucket of ice water over your head. No warning. Just splash.

"Parole? For what?" I mean, if it was something like breaking and entering to rescue a child out of a burning building, that was one thing. Homicide, however, was another. I'd have to think about how justifiable the homicide was, such as answering a cell phone during a movie, before considering marrying a man who had to file paperwork every time he left the country.

Still, what kind of murderous maniac volunteers at an animal shelter? He couldn't be all bad, right? Unless he was planning to weaponize kittens.

"He didn't say, and I didn't ask." She stacked a pile of folders neatly into the completed orders box. "Thank goodness I have a boyfriend. Who's not on parole."

This day just kept getting weirder and weirder. Changing the subject, I filled Vanessa in on Mrs. Meece's visit. Her eyes bugged out.

"Margot actually called her a stupid, clueless bimbo?"

"Twice. I thought Mrs. Meece was going to have a cow. I've never seen her so angry." Come to think of it, I'd never seen her angry at all. She *was* a little clueless, but so were many other wealthy benefactors. Didn't matter. Mrs. Meece had a big heart for animals, and she wrote checks with lots of zeros, which made her quirks forgivable.

Vanessa shook her head. "If the board hears about this, which I'm sure they will, that may be the end of Margot."

"One could only dream." I'd only spent a few hours in Margot's presence, and already I was wondering if OSHA had rules about toxic bosses.

"Mrs. Meece practically single-handedly keeps this shelter afloat." Vanessa tapped her chin, thinking. "Wait! I remember the lady who brought in the scruffy dog. I was in the lobby when she came in. Margot practically kicked her out, and I know we had space available."

"Vanessa, what is going on? When I took the dog to the kennel, I noticed the runs are full of purebreds. I didn't see a mutt in the mix. Is Margot turning away dogs without pedigrees?"

"It would appear that way." Van nibbled on her lower lip. "Also, I'm not positive, but I think she raised the adoption fees. Remind me to check with Dory. Maybe Margot thinks she can make more money from purebreds."

I blew out a breath. "Great. So, we're a boutique dog shelter now? That's not exactly the point of a stray animal shelter."

"The last surgery is sedated. Do you want—"

A loud commotion in the hall cut off Vanessa's sentence. We shot each other a look and raced toward the noise.

A mountain of a man loomed over poor Dory like a thundercloud ready to drop hailstones. "What do you mean he isn't here? I *know* Percy was brought in here last week. My neighbor was watching him while I was out of town, and he accidentally left the gate open. Another neighbor saw your van pick him up by the Seven-Eleven. He called, but kept getting the voicemail."

Dory raised her hands as if fending off an attack, which, technically, I suppose she was. "Mr. Finkle, I'm sorry, but I can't find any record of a collie being admitted."

"Well, check the kennel instead of your blasted computer!"

"Yes, sir." Dory rose and skirted around the desk as far from the enraged man as possible. "If you'd like to have a seat—"

"No, I don't want to have a seat! I want to have my dog!"

Dory scurried away, leaving Vanessa and me standing in the blast radius of Mr. Finkle's fury. His eyes zeroed in on us. "Do *you* know anything about a collie that was brought in last Wednesday?"

I shook my head and squeaked, "Sorry, I wasn't here last week."

Vanessa just stood like a deer in the headlights. I nudged her. "No," she whispered.

An uncomfortable silence ensued. After what seemed like an eternity, although it was probably only five minutes, Dory emerged with the same look you'd have if someone told you to deliver bad news to a mafia boss. Her face practically screamed, *Please, don't shoot the messenger.*

"I'm sorry, Mr. Finkle," she said, voice wobbling. "We don't have a collie. Did you check with the shelter downtown?"

He banged a meaty hand down on her desk hard enough to rattle the doggy treat jar, making all of us jump like nervous chihuahuas. "My neighbor distinctly saw a woman wearing a shirt with *your* logo on it pick him up. What have you done with my dog?"

"Let me get the director for you," I said helpfully. After all, Margot got the big bucks to deal with these issues, not Dory, the volunteer.

I made a beeline to Margot's office, where— surprise, surprise—she was pretending not to hear the verbal earthquake shaking the lobby. Mr. Finkle's voice carried through the walls like an air raid siren.

"Yes?" Margot finally looked up from a notebook, her face pinched in irritation.

"I think you need to come to the lobby and talk to this man," I said. "He says we picked up his dog last week, but there's no record of it."

"Oh, for the love of . . ." Margot huffed out, banging the notebook down on the desk. "Am I the *only* competent person around here?"

Perhaps now was not the best time to take a vote, although I pretty much knew how *I* would vote.

She tromped out to the lobby. I followed closely like an anxious page following a queen into battle.

"What's the problem?" she barked at the unhappy Mr. Finkle. Not a hint of customer-friendly charm. Frances would've at least offered him a tissue to mop the rage-sweat from his brow.

"You people took my dog, and I want him back!"

Margot's lip curled. "Look, Mister, if we don't have a record of your dog, we don't *have* your dog. What part of that do you not understand?"

The man's red face deepened from crimson to eggplant, and I silently prayed we wouldn't need an AED for him in the lobby. I didn't treat people.

"My neighbor said he saw a blonde woman pick up my collie late at night. You're the only blonde I see around here."

He advanced on Margot, who stood her ground like she had a steel rod up her spine. I had to admire her moxie. She fixed him with a malevolent glare that would have melted the steel rod up her spine.

"I never picked up a collie. Now get out of here before I call the police."

"You go ahead and call the police!" He took another step closer until their noses almost touched. "I'll tell them how you stole my dog. Then I'm calling a lawyer and suing this place and you personally. You're going down, lady."

Margot squared her shoulders. Planting a hand square on his chest, she gave a shove. Hard. "Get out of here, you deranged lunatic."

He stumbled backward, his fists shooting up— then hesitated, apparently realizing that clocking a woman in front of a crowd of witnesses wasn't the winning legal strategy he hoped to achieve.

Lowering his hands, he snapped, "You haven't heard the last of this. You stole my dog, and I will do whatever it takes to get him back. You got that, lady? Whatever. It. Takes."

I released the breath I hadn't realized I'd been holding when Mr. Finkle finally stormed out of the building.

Margot's eyes swept over us like a heat-seeking missile. "Don't you all have work to do?"

We scattered like cockroaches under a suddenly bright light while she pivoted on her heel and marched back to her office.

Chapter Four

I finished the last surgery and performed exams on all the new dogs, still perplexed that Mrs. Meece's mutt was the only one without a pedigree. Something smelled fishy, and it wasn't the kibble. I was going to get to the bottom of it.

Steeling my resolve, I started for the office—only to get shoulder-checked into the wall like a hockey puck by none other than Mrytle Quackenbush, barreling down the hallway. Dory raced along behind her, wringing her hands and crying, "Please, Mrs. Quackenbush, let me tell her you're here first."

Mrs. Quakenbush ignored Dory and plowed ahead like a Sherman tank in orthopedic shoes, each stomp rattling the picture frames as if we were in the middle of a minor earthquake. I had no choice but to follow the wreckage.

She didn't stop until she was towering over Margot's desk. Margot, wide-eyed, shoved her chair back so hard it squeaked in protest against the wall.

"What—" Margot rose, going on the offensive and regaining her haughty countenance quickly, but the large woman cut her off.

"You stay away from my husband!" Myrtle Quakenbush bellowed, loud enough to set off a barking chorus from the kennel.

For once, Margot appeared to be speechless.

"That's right, you home-wrecking little hussy. I know all about you and my Stanley."

Margot's eyes bugged out. "Are you out of your mind?"

"I know about your late-night meetings and how you got this job." Mrs. Quackenbush's nostrils flared like a charging bull. If it weren't for the desk between them, I had no doubt she would have charged.

Margot, to her credit, took a step closer and unleashed a laugh sharp enough to cut glass. "Do you honestly think I would stoop to having an affair with your husband?"

The older woman's chin trembled, and for a moment, I thought she was going to cry. "I know how women like you operate. Twisting vulnerable men around your little fingers, making them take leave of their senses and forget the wife who has stood by their side through thick and thin for over forty years."

Margot rolled her eyes in a way that my mother had warned me not to, for fear they might get stuck. "Mrs. Quackenbush, I assure you, the only thing going on between Stanley and me is business. He is helping me get this shelter back on track, where it needs to be."

A little wind seemed to go out of Mrytle's sails. "Then how do you explain why he hired you?"

Ooh. I was interested in learning that detail, as well. I leaned in.

Margot huffed. "Because I'm an experienced, qualified shelter manager. We met at a Chamber of Commerce breakfast last year, and I mentioned that I worked at the Flint County Animal Shelter. He called me after Frances resigned and asked if I would be interested in the job. End of story."

Mrytle's lips quivered, and a single tear escaped from her right eye and slid down her chubby, wrinkled cheek. "Do you swear you're telling me the truth?"

"Yes, of course," Margot said, irritation coloring her tone. "Stanley has eyes only for you, Mrytle." The words left her mouth as though they revolted her.

The older lady sniffled and reached a finger to her face to wipe away the tear. "Well . . . okay."

"I won't mention our little talk to Stanley," Margot said.

"I appreciate that," Mrytle whispered, clutching her purse like a life preserver. She turned to go, ignoring Dory and me pressed against the doorframe like rubberneckers at a train wreck. We took a quick step back.

"As if I couldn't do better than that old goat," Margot muttered.

Unfortunately, Margot muttered like most people shout. Her words carried loud and clear into the hallway. Mrs. Quackenbush stopped short, then executed a surprising nimble pivot for a woman her size.

"What did you just say?"

Margot frowned. "I didn't say anything."

"Yes, you did." Mrytle took another step toward Margot. "You called my Stanley an old goat."

Margot's lips tightened. "So what if I did? If I were going to seduce somebody's husband, do you honestly think I'd pick yours?" She barked out a laugh. "Please. I'm not that desperate."

Mrytle's mouth opened and closed several times like a fish out of water. Finally, she squeaked out, "And why not? What's wrong with my Stanley?" Her jowls quivered with enough force to register on the Richter scale.

Margot smacked a hand to her forehead. "Did you seriously just ask me that question? First, your knickers are in a knot because you think I want to have an affair with your husband, and now they're in a knot because you think I don't." She shook her head. "I'll tell you something, you stupid old cow." She jabbed a finger in Mrytle's direction. "You and your old goat were meant for each other. You deserve each other."

Mrs. Quackenbush let out a strangled cry, pressed her fist to her mouth, and skedaddled out of the building faster than I'd ever seen such a large woman move.

The dust hadn't even settled when Margot's eyes once again speared me. I glanced around, but Dory had disappeared along with Mrs. Quackenbush.

"What?" Margot snapped.

I reconsidered my approach to rationally speaking to her at this particular time. "Uh, nothing. I'll talk to you later."

Making a hasty exit, I headed back toward the lobby, rehearsing the tongue-lashing I planned to deliver to Dory for abandoning me. But the phone's shrill ring cut through my righteous fury.

"Answer the d~ phone!" screeched Merlin.

I skidded to a stop like someone had yanked my leash, my eyes rounding in disbelief. I shot a look at Dory, who wore the world's worst poker face. She slapped a hand over the receiver and whispered, "He's learned a lot of new phrases."

"New phrases?" My voice cracked. "That one belongs in the 'absolutely not' vocabulary for an official greeter." I leaned toward the bird, wagging a finger like I was scolding a feathery toddler. "Merlin, sweetie, let's try this instead: 'Thank you. Have a nice day.'"

He puffed up his feathers like a feather duster and stretched out his wings. "My shelter, my rules."

I folded my arms. "Thank you. Have a nice day."

The bird peered at me through beady eyes.

I sighed. Either Merlin would need some serious deprogramming or a demotion to the break room. Maybe even the supply closet, where no one could hear him.

Before I could head back into surgery, the kennel door opened, and Robert Redford, aka Kip Gallagher—who could tell the difference with that smile—stepped out holding a dog.

"Well, what do you think?" His mega-watt grin lit up the room, complete with a dimple I hadn't noticed earlier.

Drat. I really needed to know what crime had landed him in the pokey and whether it was something I could overlook.

I managed to drag my eyes from his face to the dog and tried to focus. "What do I think about what?"

"Bruno. I cleaned him up and shaved the mats."

I did a double-take. Mrs. Meece's scruffy mystery mutt had morphed into a surprisingly cute curly-coated brown dog with big, Precious Moment eyes.

"Wow! It doesn't look like the same dog."

"Looks can be deceiving," said Kip.

My brow creased. Was that remark about the dog or himself? Plenty of serial killers were good-looking. Some probably had dimples. Nope. Not going there. "Uh, Bruno?"

Kip nuzzled the dog, a pure look of adoration on his face. "Yeah. I figured the little guy had a rough start. He needed a macho name to make up for it."

My brain short-circuited. How could an ex-con be such an animal softie? His crime had to be something tame—Embezzlement? Insurance fraud? Shoplifting cupcakes?

"He's ready for his intake exam."

"Huh?"

Kip arched a brow. "His exam?"

Focus, Amanda. I cleared my throat, which suddenly had my heart clogging it. "Yes, of course. Let's take him into surgery."

I led the way, acutely aware of Kip behind me. Once inside, I directed Kip to put Bruno on the table while I drew up vaccines and opened a heartworm test, which my butterfingers flung to the floor. *Smooth move, competent doggie doctor.*

As I stooped to retrieve the test, Vanessa emerged from the post-op area, her eyes darting between the two of us. "I've got this," she said, swooping in to take the dog and practically shoving Kip toward the door. "I'll bring him back when we're done."

Kip shrugged, dimple flashing, and slipped out, closing the door behind him.

I whirled on Vanessa. "Why did you do that?"

"Do what?"

"You were rude to Kip. You basically kicked him out of the room."

"I did not. I'm the tech, remember? It's my job."

"He was only holding the dog for me. I didn't know where you were."

"You might have tried to call, 'Vanessa, are you in here? I need some help,' instead of dragging in Mr. Mugshot."

I huffed, then bent over Bruno, determined to bury my irritation under medical professionalism.

"Besides," Vanessa added. "You shouldn't be in here alone with that man."

My head snapped up. "What? Why? Do you think he has an axe hidden in his scrubs that he intends to hack me to death with?"

Her chin shot up. "I just don't trust him. Who knows what he did? So, sue me for trying to protect you."

"Van, you're being judgmental. He's paid his debt to society. He deserves a chance to be . . . whatever." I stuck my stethoscope into my ears so I didn't have to listen to her rebuttal. It might have been childish, but I really didn't want to have this discussion. I spent an exaggerated amount of time listening to Bruno's heartbeat. Strong. Solid. Trustworthy. I wish I could confidently say the same about Kip Gallagher.

Chapter Five

It had been a long, grueling, eye-opening day, and I needed to escape before my brain melted into a puddle on the floor. But first, I had to confront Margot—the conversation I'd been putting off all afternoon.

As I passed through the lobby, Merlin called out, "This place is a mess!"

"Yes, it is," I replied, "but not in the way you think."

"Shut the door, genius! Were you born in a barn?"

"Merlin, you'd better knock it off, or it's the linen closet for you."

I continued down the hall to Margot's office. She sat hunched over a large folder that she quickly stuffed into her top drawer before glowering at me. At least she'd stayed out of my way for the afternoon, for which I thanked the Lord for small mercies.

"What?" she snapped.

I sighed. Her disposition hadn't improved with the passing hours. Still, I suppose if at least three people had chewed me out in the past few hours, I might be a tad bit cranky, too. I plopped into the seat across from her without invitation and said, "I'd like a minute of your time."

She made a show of consulting her watch. "A minute is all I have. Make it quick."

"Margot—" I stopped when I saw her narrowed eyes, quickly realizing my faux pas. "Sorry, Ms. Dilly. I can't help but notice that with the exception of Mrs. Meece's stray, every dog here is a purebred."

"So?" Her eyes challenged me to make my point.

"Well, that's unusual for a shelter. Purebreds are usually the exception."

"We've had a lot of surrenders lately. I have no control over what comes in." She busied herself with rearranging pens in a coffee mug that said, "I'm not bossy. I'm *the* boss."

"But you told Mrs. Meece that there wasn't room for her stray. And there are several open runs."

"That was *last* week when you weren't here, and we were full. Now, are you finished telling me how to run my shelter?" She started to rise.

My backbone stiffened. "No. I want to know what's going on around here."

Her lips curved downward in a slow, theatrical frown. "What's going on," she said, in a tone one would use for an exceptionally dense person, "is that I inherited a shelter that's bleeding red ink and being run in a slipshod manner, and I'm trying to fix it. If you don't like the way I run this place, you're free to leave."

Anger burned in my stomach. "Mar . . . Ms. Dilly, I don't see how making people mad and questioning our practices is helping. Antagonizing the staff isn't helping either. The staff is not happy, and frankly, neither am I. I'm a professional who has gladly donated my time and services to this shelter, but rather than showing appreciation, you've done nothing but find fault with me."

Her face pinched. "Fine. Then you're fired."

My mouth dropped open, and the anger crept up my throat into my voice. "What? You can't fire me. I'm a volunteer!" I stood, shoving the chair back with more force than I intended, grabbing it before it toppled over.

"I quit!" I shouted, my voice echoing off the walls.

"Don't let the door hit you on the way out," she muttered.

I stomped down the hall, through the lobby, and out the front door, fighting the burning tears in my eyes. Stopping on the sidewalk to haul in a long breath, I jumped when the door behind me opened. I turned to see Kip.

"Are you okay?" he asked, concern and charm oozing from his dreamy eyes.

Sniffling, I nodded and huffed out a cheerless laugh. "Margot just *fired* me. Can you believe it?"

"I heard raised voices. But then again, yelling is Margot's love language." He smirked.

His comment made me snort in a rather unladylike manner. "I have never been fired from a job in my life. *Especially* a volunteer job."

"Well, I wouldn't worry too much about it. Where are they going to find a vet who works for free?"

I drew in a calming breath. "That's just it, Kip. I care about this place. I believe in what I do here. I want to make a difference." I shook my head and chuckled. "And you're right. Not many vets are willing to give up a day off to do this."

He placed a tentative hand on my shoulder, and sparks raced from my neck to my toes. I almost shrieked from the electricity.

"I'll bet it won't be long before she begs you to come back." He winked at me, and my knees turned to rubber. "At double the salary."

I couldn't help but let out a full-fledged belly laugh. Wiping my moist eyes, I said, "You're probably right. Thanks. And thanks for cleaning up Bruno. That was really sweet."

He finally removed his hand, leaving a cold void on my shoulder. Shrugging, he said, "It's the least I could do for the poor little guy."

I turned questioning eyes to him. "Margot has managed to alienate everyone else at the shelter. How do you get along with her?"

He shrugged again. "I just let her nastiness roll off me and do my job. I like my work, and I love the animals. So, I tune her out."

"Hmph. That's easier said than done."

His expression changed, and his eyes turned serious. "So," he said, dropping his gaze. "Would you like to grab a burger or something? You can unload all your bad day on me. I'm a good listener."

Although my heart did cartwheels against my ribs, I hesitated, Vanessa's warnings ringing loudly in my ears.

Kip caught my hesitation, understanding evident on his face. "It's okay, maybe another time." He turned to go.

"Oh, no, wait. You don't understand."

He paused, expectant.

I glanced at my watch. "It's just that I have choir practice tonight. And I'm already late."

He tilted his head. Disbelief colored his expression. "Right. Choir practice. Whatever."

My heart stopped its acrobatics and thudded like a rock to the bottom of my chest as I watched him head back into the building.

Chapter Six

The thing was, I wasn't lying to Kip. I really did have choir practice, and I really was late—which meant the only open chair was next to Stella Ramsey. Stella, bless her heart, was tone deaf. In the way a foghorn is tone deaf. But what she lacked in pitch, she more than made up for in volume.

I could usually hold my own musically. I knew my part. I could read notes and carry a tune in a bucket. But put me next to Stella, and suddenly the bucket had holes. Not only couldn't I find my note, but I couldn't even hear myself think, let alone sing. Naturally, the earlier arrivals had all abandoned the Stella zone, scooting down the row and leaving me as the sacrificial lamb.

Still, I reminded myself, our little choir wasn't auditioning for a European cathedral tour. And the Scripture did say to make a joyful noise unto the Lord. Despite her lack of musical ability, Stella delivered on the noise front. If enthusiasm earned heavenly crowns, she'd be wearing a tiara the size of Texas. My heart, however, needed an attitude adjustment because while Stella was busy with heartfelt worship, I kept wishing she'd come down with laryngitis.

Our choir director, Faith—which I always thought was a fitting name for someone in the ministry—acknowledged me with a nod and a knowing grin. I quickly found my place and joined in the anthem, singing alto because no one else in the choir could read music.

We hadn't gotten through a half page when Faith clapped her hands and signaled for us to stop. "Remember, people, to cut off that last note after four counts. Watch me. I will cut you off."

Stella, aside from being tone deaf, also couldn't count to four when it came to music. Everyone knew Faith referred to Stella, but dear, sweet Faith never singled out individuals, which was both a blessing and a curse. Everyone but Stella knew she always belted her way into the next measure like a Lone Ranger soloist, and nothing would ever change.

Not that it mattered. After Sunday service, the congregation would beam and tell us how beautiful we sounded, in the same way a mother pats her kid on the head and declares his finger painting a masterpiece before hanging it on the refrigerator. We all knew better, but hey—love covers a multitude of sins. Especially musical ones.

I had arrived just in time for the break.

"Did you get stuck working late at the shelter tonight?" asked Laurie, a soprano with a beautiful, but unfortunately soft voice, as I uncapped a water bottle and downed a large gulp.

I wiped my hand across my mouth. "Yes. It was quite a day." I didn't want to go into detail, but another woman, Kay, pushed into the conversation.

"What's up with that new director?" Kay asked. "I went by there last week looking for my daughter's lost cat, and that woman was extremely rude to me. Told me I should have called first because I was disrupting the schedule. Since when do animal shelters have schedules?" Kay looked around and lowered her voice. "And that parrot in the front office propositioned me."

Oh no. I groaned. "What did he say?" Then I held up my hand like a stop sign. "You know what? I really don't want to know."

Yolanda, who never missed a chance to stir the pot, jumped into the conversation. "I heard that the new director, Margot, is having an affair with Commissioner Quackenbush. That's how she got the job." She crossed her arms and looked as smug as a cat sitting on a freshly folded laundry pile.

"Really?" Kay and Laurie harmonized in perfect union—better than they had all night, incidentally. Their eyes popped wide as they leaned in, practically salivating over the gossip tidbit.

"Ladies," I said, shooting them an admonishing look. "I don't think that rumor is true, and honestly, we shouldn't be discussing this in church." Or anywhere, for that matter. Not that I was above a little morsel of gossip myself, but that particular story needed to die before it sprouted wings and took flight.

"Stanley Quackenbush?" Kay persisted, ignoring my attempt at righteousness. "No job is worth that."

Before I had to wrestle them all back to spiritual ground, Faith called us back to practice, saving me from becoming the Choir Gossip Police.

After choir practice broke up, Kay's earlier comment about her daughter's missing cat nagged at me. I couldn't leave without knowing the outcome. Lost animals weighed heavily on my heart.

"Kay," I called, trotting to catch up with her in the parking lot. "Did your daughter ever find her cat?"

"Huh?" Kay gave me a confused look, then laughed. "Oh, yes. He wandered home the next day. She tries to keep him inside, but the little bugger could escape from Alcatraz." She thought that statement over for a moment and then added, "Well, maybe not. Cats don't like water."

"I'm glad," I said, relief washing over me. I wouldn't have been able to sleep tonight, not knowing the fate of Kay's grand-kitty.

"Have a good day at work tomorrow," she said as she opened her car door.

"Thanks." I headed for my own car, my thoughts already fast-forwarding to my first day back at the clinic after my month-long absence. Then, I suddenly remembered I had left my stethoscope at the shelter. Shoot! Sure, I could have used one of the many stethoscopes lying all over the hospital, but mine was like a pair of old sneakers—broken in, comfortable, and irreplaceable. Besides, I would have to fetch it sooner or later, and it was unlikely anyone would be there this late, sparing me another potential encounter with the wicked witch of the shelter.

I drove back to the shelter, pulling into the well-lit front lot because the back was dark and creepy. Fortunately, Margot hadn't asked for my key. I unlocked the door and started for the surgery area when I heard voices coming from Margot's office. Naturally, I had to investigate.

Creeping closer, I pressed a finger to my lips and shot Merlin a warning not to rat me out.

"Stupid bimbo," he squawked.

I gritted my teeth. If parrots could smirk, that bird would be doing it.

"I told you on the phone, Stanley, the golf tournament didn't bring in that much money." Margot's voice. "What do you want me to do? I can't get blood out of a turnip."

Another voice growled back, garbled like it was being filtered through a mouthful of gravel—or in this case, a cigar. "Not buying it, Margot. Golf tournaments always generate big money."

The faint stench of smoke rolled down the hallway, and my blood pressure spiked. The shelter was a smoke-free facility for a reason. But, of course, rules didn't extend to big-shot politicians, even though they were only county commissioners of a small county.

"Well, this time it didn't," Margot snapped. "Your cut is one thousand dollars. Take it or leave it."

I gasped out loud and clamped a hand over my mouth. So *that* was the connection between Margot and Stanley. Greed. Pure, old-fashioned, animals-be-darned corruption.

It took all my self-control not to barge in there and confront the two. But that action wouldn't do any good. It would be my word against theirs. Besides, what would they do to me if they found me eavesdropping? I pressed against the wall, praying my heart didn't drum loud enough to give me away.

"This next fundraiser better be more lucrative," he snarled. "Or I may need to find someone else for your position."

"Be my guest, you old windbag. You can't afford to lose me. Besides, I have a big mouth."

"Don't threaten me, Margot. Just do what we agreed on, and we'll both be happy. Got it?"

"It's late. Go home, Stanley. Or Mrytle may accuse me of seducing you again."

He gave a loud *harumph*.

"And be sure to go out the back. We don't need anyone seeing you here."

"I'm not stupid, Margot. Where do you think I parked?"

Too terrified to move, I pressed myself against the wall and closed my eyes. The back door creaked open and slammed shut, and a couple of minutes later, the lights clicked off in Margot's office. I exhaled, slinking to the surgery room like a burglar in scrubs, and ducked inside, praying she wouldn't come this way. Shortly afterward, I heard the back door open and close again.

I waited a few more minutes, giving my galloping heart rate and breathing time to recover. Then I groped around the surgery room for my stethoscope, too afraid to turn on the lights, lest Margot see them and come back to investigate.

Finally, I eased my way back to the lobby, freezing once again when I saw light spilling out into the hallway from the office. I knew I should have high-tailed it out the front door, but curiosity got the better of me. Yeah, I know what they say about curiosity and the cat. But now that I knew for sure something shaky was going on, perhaps I could get more proof. And I might not have another opportunity.

Once more, I crept toward the office, but this time, I craned my neck to see around the corner. My heart lurched. Kip Gallagher sat at Margot's desk, rummaging through open drawers like a raccoon through a trash can.

Fantastic. An ex-con in an empty shelter office late at night. What could possibly go wrong?

The fact that I was alone in a building with a man who might or might not be a serial killer barely entered my mind as I stepped boldly into the office and demanded, "What are you doing?"

He jumped, and papers went flying. "Amanda? What are you doing here?" He stooped to gather up the scattered papers.

Hah! He thought he could turn the tables on me by going on the offensive. Nice try, but not going to work. I raised the hand holding the stethoscope like Exhibit A. "I forgot this. What did *you* forget?"

He scrambled for a grin. *Nope, Robert, don't even try dialing up the charm.* I thrust my hands on my hips.

"I forgot to give Margot the intake form for Brutus."

I folded my arms. "You could have left it on her desk."

Kip forced out an unconvincing laugh. "Well, to be honest, I've been remiss in all my paperwork. I wanted to get everything filed properly before Margot discovered my deficiencies."

I shook my head. "You're a poor liar."

His jaw tightened. "Oh, so the guy on parole must be in here for criminal purposes. Just what do you think I'm doing, Amanda? Running an underground hamster-fighting ring? Smuggling black market catnip? The *good* stuff?" His gorgeous blue eyes flared.

"You shouldn't be in here." Then, against all my better judgment, I said, "And just what *were* you in the joint for, anyway?" I didn't know if I'd used the right slang for "prison," but I didn't care.

Without batting an eye, he said, "Three to five."

"What?" I said, momentarily taken aback.

"Three to five," he repeated. "I got paroled early for good behavior. Any other questions?"

Okay, he'd won that round. He wasn't giving up any information. I chewed on my top lip. "I should report you to Margot," I said, but even to me, the threat sounded weak.

He raised his brows. "But we both know you won't. Because then you'll have to explain what *you're* doing here. And she might put two and two together and realize you overheard her little exchange with Stanley Quackenbush."

For the second time that night, I gasped. So, Kip had heard everything, too.

His expression softened. "Look, Amanda, I'm not up to anything shady. You'll just have to take my word on this."

Take his word. An ex-con. Still, I knew from a few minutes ago that he was a lousy liar. I found my head nodding of its own accord. Besides, what choice did I have?

"All right," I conceded. "There's a lot of funny business going on around here. But I don't need any more drama in my life. Good night, Kip."

"Would you like me to escort you to your car?"

I almost choked on the laugh that bubbled up from deep in my gut. Could this day get any weirder? Did the ex-con seriously just ask me if I wanted him to walk me out into the dark parking lot, where he could toss me in the trunk, drive out into the middle of nowhere, and dump my dead body where no one would ever find it?

I shook my head. "No, thank you. I'm fine."

He gave me a sad smile that pricked the edges of my conscience as I turned to go.

At the front door, Merlin piped up, "Good night, sweetie."

Chapter Seven

The following day, I dragged myself into my paying job at Barkley's Animal Clinic—yes, my boss' name was Fred Barkley—feeling like I needed a vacation. Maybe Belize. Except, having just returned from Belize, that wasn't likely to happen. Funny how dodging tarantulas and sweating through scrubs in a jungle suddenly felt like a luxury spa day compared to the day I'd had yesterday.

I didn't particularly want to share my termination from my volunteer position with my coworkers. That little tidbit wasn't exactly resume material. So, I pasted on a smile and accepted the "welcome backs" and "how was your trip," and elaborated on my adventure to anyone who would listen. But before I could show off the 953 photos on my phone, work intervened, and my audience began to dwindle. Surely, it was difficult to tear themselves away.

I groaned at the mess that had accumulated on my desk in my absence. Oscar, the clinic cat, twitched an ear from his sunbeam that fell across the clutter. Stacks of patient files with sticky notes attached, prescription refill requests, and a urine sample in a cup—please, God, let it be a fresh one—sat next to a sympathy card that should've been mailed before I left. Oscar lounged on a pile of unopened mail, and a shelter donation jar stuffed with coins glinted at me like pirate treasure.

I set the donation jar aside. No way was I going to let Commissioner Quackenbush and Margot get their grubby paws on the assortment of coins that was designated for animal care. If nothing else, I would take the money, hit the nearest pet store, and deliver kibble and chew toys to the shelter's doorstep under the cover of darkness like a benevolent cat burglar.

As I shuffled my way through pet product catalogues and professional journals, my technician, Tiffany, knocked on the door.

"Your first patient is here," she announced.

Happy to leave the avalanche behind, I took the chart she held out, eager to get to work. Oscar scooted back onto the pile of mail I had been sorting, kicked some to the floor, and curled up, fixing me with a territorial eye.

Tiffany briefed me as we walked to the first exam room. "It's a new pet exam. The lady just got him from the shelter over the weekend. She wants to have him microchipped."

Good. Something relatively uncomplicated to ease me back into my routine. A happy new owner and a healthy dog.

I opened the exam room door to see an attractive middle-aged woman and a handsome collie with a white ruff and soulful brown eyes.

"Hello," I greeted, holding out my hand. "I'm Dr. Reynolds."

"Lola Huxley," the woman replied warmly, giving my hand a shake. "And this is Cedric. I couldn't believe my good fortune at finding him." She beamed at the beautiful animal. "My old collie, Laddie, passed away after twelve wonderful years. I thought I'd check the shelter on a whim. I didn't expect to find a collie, but thought it was worth a try."

"What a nice-looking dog. I'm surprised he was at a shelter. Which shelter was it?" I crouched to give Cedric's noble head a rub.

A puzzled look crossed her face. "Why, the county shelter. You were the one who signed the intake papers. That's why I came here, since you already know Cedric. Don't you remember him?"

I stood, frowning. "No, you must be mistaken. I've been gone for a month. I haven't seen any coll . . ." I felt the blood draining from my face. "May I see your paperwork?"

"Yes, of course." She reached into a large tote bag and pulled out a folder. "Here is everything the shelter gave me." As I took the folder from her hand, she continued. "I stopped in last week, asking if they had any collies. The very nice lady I talked to said she would keep an eye out for me, and would you believe it? Two days later, she called me and said they'd just had a collie surrendered. She even stayed late so I could pick him up."

Her words floated over me as I flipped through the pages. At the very back, I found what I was looking for—Cedric's intake form with his physical exam, lab work, and vaccines filled in and signed by Dr. Amanda Reynolds. My name and my signature. Except it wasn't. My heart somersaulted and fell flat against my diaphragm. Margot had forged my signature!

"Mrs. Huxley, tell me again. Where did the woman at the shelter say Cedric came from?"

Her brows knitted with confusion. "She said someone had just surrendered him right before they closed. She remembered I was looking for a collie, and she called me immediately. She waited for me so I could take him right away because she didn't want him admitted to the shelter, where he might be exposed to something from the other dogs."

"And when was this?" I continued to stare at the falsified form in disbelief.

"Friday night. Is something wrong?" She placed a protective hand on the dog.

"May I ask what you paid for the adoption fee?"

She hesitated. "Five hundred dollars." A worried expression replaced her confusion.

"Five hundred!" The pit of my stomach fluttered as my mind replayed the confrontation Mr. Finkle had had with Margot yesterday. I decided to try a little experiment. "Percy!"

The dog's head shot up, and his tail wagged furiously as he bounded over to wash my face with kisses.

My throat tightened. I turned to Mrs. Huxley and laid a gentle hand on hers. "Mrs. Huxley, I'm afraid this dog may have been stolen. I think this dog is named Percy, and he belongs to a man named Mr. Finkle."

"Stolen!" Her face paled.

"Yes." I opened the exam room door and called for Tiffany.

Mrs. Huxley's lower lip quivered. "Oh dear. I knew that finding a beautiful dog like this was too good to be true." Tears glistened in her eyes.

Tiffany appeared at the door.

"Would you please scan this dog for a microchip?" I asked. Tiffany nodded and left to retrieve the scanner.

"So if he has a microchip, does that mean he's stolen?"

"Not necessarily. Nor does the lack of a microchip prove he isn't. But there are a few things I need to tell you." I guided her to the chairs and sat next to her. Pointing to the forged intake form, I said, "This is not my signature. I was out of the country on this date."

Tears escaped and trickled down her cheeks.

"Yesterday, I worked at the shelter, and Mr. Finkle came in looking for his collie that had gotten out by accident. He told the director, Margot Dilly, that a neighbor had seen her pick up the dog. She told him she hadn't picked up any collies."

"Margot Dilly. That was her name." Mrs. Huxley took out a tissue and blew her nose. "And she seemed like such a nice young woman."

"Not only that, but our adoption fee is only $150." I didn't want to speculate aloud as to what I now believed was going on, but the puzzle pieces began to click together in my head. Margot was flipping through purebreds like used cars, raking in fat fees and splitting the profits with her good buddy, Commissioner Quackenbush.

Tiffany returned and ran the scanner over Cedric. It emitted a loud beep. "Yep, he already has a chip. I'll see if I can trace the number."

I took the woman's hand. "I'm sorry, Mrs. Huxley."

"I've already grown attached to him." She sniffled and forced out a watery smile. "But I certainly don't want to keep a dog who belongs to someone else."

"Let me see if we can get this straightened out," I said.

I left the disconsolate woman with Percy-Cedric, dabbing her eyes, and hovered over Tiffany, who had the phone pressed to her ear while furiously writing on a pad. "Uh, huh. Uh, huh. Thank you."

She hung up and shoved the pad at me. "The dog belongs to Jerome Finkle. I have his information here."

I pressed my lips together and nodded. "I'll go break the news to Mrs. Huxley."

Mrs. Huxley waited until Mr. Finkle arrived twenty minutes later, and the moment he stepped inside, Percy went ballistic. The dog practically lunged across the room, spinning in circles, barking as if he had just won the lottery. There was no question who owned him.

Jerome Finkle's emotions bounced all over the place—from a tearful relief at being reunited with his dog to thunderous rage at Margot's deception.

"I apologize again, Mr. Finkle," said Mrs. Huxley. "I had no idea this dog belonged to someone." The woman had not stopped expressing her regret since Percy's owner appeared. One would have thought she was Margot's partner in crime.

"It's not your fault," I repeated for the umpteenth time. "You didn't know."

"Just wait until I get my hands on that lying broad. She'll be sorry she ever dared to mess with my dog and me." Finkle's face had once more turned a shade of red I didn't know existed, and I feared for his blood pressure.

"Mr. Finkle," I said, trying to calm him down before he suffered a stroke, and Percy ended up going home with Mrs. Huxley after all. "We have enough on Margot to go to the police. With her forging professional documents and stealing animals, she's crossed the line from suspicious behavior into outright criminal activity."

A vision of Margot in an orange jumpsuit sprang to mind, and I had to admit, I liked it. Orange was so not her color. And although I didn't mention Stanley Quackenbush's involvement, I wanted to see him go down with her. A public servant who abused public trust deserved no less. He wouldn't look good in orange either.

Mr. Finkle finally left, after promising not to throttle Margot and end up in the slammer, himself. He even reimbursed Mrs. Huxley the five hundred dollars she'd paid Margot. "But I'm filing a complaint with the police," he growled.

"That's an excellent plan, Mr. Finkle," I said. "I'm planning on doing the same."

But with the Percy drama eating up half my day—and the rest consumed with a mountain of paperwork and an endless parade of sick patients—I fell way behind. The day passed in a blur, pushing Margot's impending incarceration to the mental folder labeled "To do later."

By the time the day ended, I still hadn't called the police. Perhaps it would be better to stop by the precinct on my way home and talk to someone in person. I walked to my car and started the engine, my brain finally free to untangle the past twenty-four hours. Thoughts chased each other through my mind, not the least of which was Margot forging my name. My professional license and livelihood, not to mention my sanity, were on the line, something I didn't take lightly.

As I drove along, my anger mounted. So, when I passed by the shelter on my way to the police station and saw Margot's car out front, something inside me snapped. I didn't have to worry about Mr. Finkle throttling Margot. I intended to handle that job all by myself.

Chapter Eight

I **didn't stop** to wonder why Margot had parked out front instead of in the back parking lot. I just knew that the sight of her car beckoned me like a siren luring sailors to their death. Fury drove me forward as I whipped into the spot beside her, grabbed Percy's folder from the passenger seat, and stormed through the front door.

A fog of anger wrapped itself around me like a strangling cloak. I stomped down the hall like a one-woman band of storm troopers marching to Margot's office, where she sat with her back to the door.

A traveling cage, with Merlin inside, rested on the table next to her desk. He let out a wolf whistle and called, "Hello, beautiful."

In my peripheral thoughts, I wondered why Merlin was in the office, but my more urgent matter commanded full attention, and even Merlin's cheerful greeting didn't lift my spirits or detract from my mission.

"Margot!" I barked. "I know everything!" At least I thought I knew everything, but it sounded good. I slammed the folder on the desk. "You made a huge mistake by forging my name on official documents. I'm going to see to it that you're prosecuted to the full extent of the law."

She didn't flinch. Didn't acknowledge me. She didn't even turn around, which stoked my fire even hotter.

"Margot! Look at me when I'm yelling at you!" When she still didn't respond, I marched around the desk, grabbed her chair, and spun it like I was auditioning for *Wheel of Fortune.*

That's when I screamed and jumped back in horror. Margot's unblinking, buggy eyes stared out at me from her purple face with no trace of the smug defiance she'd worn in life. A blue nylon leash with the words "Dalton County Animal Shelter" was cinched around her neck like some macabre accessory. I stood frozen in the unnaturally silent room. It seemed the very air held its breath. The metallic tang of panic rose in my throat, and I realized with a jolt that the killer might still be here.

As if on cue, Kip burst into the room, and I screamed again. Backing away into the wall, I held up my hands as though they would make me bulletproof. "Please, don't hurt me. I have a cat at home. She depends on me." I lowered my head and covered it with my arms with the brilliant logic that if I couldn't see him, he couldn't see me. My heart skittered around my chest in an irregular cadence, like a hamster on an exercise wheel. Any second now, I was sure it would give out. But maybe, if I had a heart attack right now, I would be spared the fate of whatever Kip had in store for me. Hadn't I suspected, deep down, that he was a serial killer?

The fact that begging for your life rarely works in scary movies flashed through my mind. Perhaps I should stop being a sitting duck and look for something to defend myself with. I peeked through my arms and searched the desk for a weapon. Scissors, a letter opener, a paperweight—even rubber bands, if my shaking fingers could shoot them straight.

"Amanda, stop! I didn't kill her." Kip raised his hands and took a cautious step toward me.

I shrieked again and cowered behind the chair, using Margot's dead body as my human shield. Okay, maybe not the classiest move, but desperate times, and all. Besides, he couldn't hurt Margot anymore.

He sighed and reached into his pocket. "I didn't want to have to do this, but—"

I panicked, snatched the cup of pens, and launched it at his head.

He dodged the cup, and the flying pens clattered across the room. "Amanda, stop! Look." He held up an official-looking badge in a case. "I'm an undercover police officer."

My heart's erratic beat stuttered, stopped for a second, then resumed at a tempo slightly less insane. "Undercover?" I squeaked. Could I trust him? Couldn't people get fake police badges online?

"How do I know that isn't a fake ID?" I desperately wanted to believe him. Otherwise, the alternative didn't look too rosy for me.

He held it out for my closer inspection. I took the case from him, keeping my eyes locked on his, while my peripheral vision scouted for a backup weapon on the desk. Daring to lower my gaze to the badge, I scrutinized it. Not that I knew what I was looking for. How does one tell an authentic badge from a fake one? I handed it back.

"You can call the police and verify that the badge is legit," he said.

I pulled in a deep breath and tried to wrestle my frazzled nerves under control. "If you're really a cop, what are you doing working undercover in an animal shelter?" I eased out from behind the chair. "Don't you have more important cases, like drug cartels, mafia, and . . ." I had been about to say "murders" until I realized I was standing next to a corpse.

He shoved the badge into his pocket and ran a hand through his hair. "We've had our eye on Margot Dilly for a few months now. But we couldn't prove anything. When she landed this job, under the suspicious appointment by Stanley Quackenbush, we decided we needed someone on the inside."

My head spun. I tried to process everything, but I found it all too overwhelming. "But why pose as an ex-con doing community service?"

"Because what grown man volunteers to clean cages at an animal shelter?"

Good point. "So, now what?" I asked.

Kip shook his head. "Now we have an entirely different situation on our hands. Which brings me to a question I need to ask you."

"What?" Something in his tone triggered my heart to do strange things again.

"I'm sorry to have to ask you this, Amanda, but what are *you* doing here?"

Oh. *Oh.* Suddenly, I had graduated from potential *victim* of a serial killer to potential killer. "I . . . uh, came by to confront her with this." I picked up the folder I had slammed on the desk and handed it to him. Before he had a chance to open it, I grabbed it back and turned to the last page. "Margot has been forging my signature on official veterinary documents. I found out today when a client brought in a dog that Margot had stolen and sold to her." I went on, my words pouring out so fast, I tripped over them, as he scanned the papers. I tried to explain what I knew about the illegal activities with Margot and Stanley. But I'm afraid my rambling only muddled the facts further.

Finally, I paused for breath and said, "Am I a suspect? Do I need a lawyer?"

I didn't know any lawyers except for Buddy Brown, who advertised "Hurt in an accident? Buddy Brown Battles Like a Bulldog," on billboards in three counties. He also owned an adorable bulldog, named Peaches, who suffered from allergies. Would Buddy represent me since I'd managed to clear up Peaches' itching? Or was homicide a little outside his wheelhouse?

Kip gave me a look I couldn't quite read. "I'm afraid everyone's a suspect until they're not. The police will certainly want to question you." He tried to soften the words with a grin. "I wouldn't be overly concerned at this point, but don't leave town."

Did the cops actually say those words? I didn't know quite how to take that statement. "Shouldn't we call the police about—" I gestured to Margot—"you know."

"Next on my list," he said, pulling out his cellphone. "You'll need to stay put, but don't touch anything."

"Can I wait in the lobby? I'd really rather not . . ." My eyes drifted back to Margot.

"Yes." He waved me off as he punched a button on his phone.

I picked up Merlin's travel crate and staggered out of the office in a daze. After releasing him back to his own cage, I sank into a plastic chair and pressed my hands to my temples. How had my day unraveled into this nightmare?

"Merlin," I mumbled, "Say something to take my mind off all this."

"Stupid bimbo."

Perfect. Exactly the pep talk I needed.

I answered the officers' questions so many times my head throbbed like I'd headbutted a brick wall. In many ways, I thought I had.

"Just once more, Dr. Reynolds," said Cop Number One, whose name I couldn't remember. He appeared to have kind eyes in a somewhat vague, interrogating way. Not kind enough for me to relax, however. Not that I had anything to hide, but with my tenancy toward verbal diarrhea, I might inadvertently confess to stealing that bottle of cat shampoo. Technically, it was already opened and couldn't be sold, but—

"You said you came here tonight to talk to Ms. Dilly about shelter records for an animal."

I blew out a frustrated breath between my lips. How many times were they going to ask me the same thing? Were they trying to trick me into contradicting myself? I knew their tactics. I watched *Law and Order*.

"Yes, for the millionth time."

"Do you often come by the shelter at night?" asked Cop Number Two, whose name I also couldn't remember.

Okay, red alert! New question. "No, but I needed to talk to Margo tonight."

"Yet you were here last night, also." Number Two's stare drilled holes through my skull.

A prickle of anxiety jabbed at my gut. How did they know that, unless . . . I whipped my head toward Kip, who sat across the room. Either he or Merlin had tattled, and somehow, I didn't think Merlin qualified as an expert witness.

"Yes," I said, working hard to keep the defensiveness out of my voice. "I'd forgotten my stethoscope."

"And you didn't see Ms. Dilly last night?"

"No." I hesitated, which I realized didn't look good for me. "Well, actually, I heard her and Commissioner Quackenbush talking." I went on to explain what I'd overheard. Then I raised my chin and fixed my eyes on Kip. "And I saw Officer Gallagher in her office, going through her desk." So there. Two could play at this ratting-out game.

Number One leaned forward, his voice smooth. "It must have upset you to learn Ms. Dilly had been signing your name to official papers."

I swallowed down my irritation and tried to speak calmly. "Of course it upset me. It's my professional reputation on the line." I held his piercing gaze, which didn't look so kind anymore.

"And it must have upset you when she fired you," said Number Two.

Whoa! Talk about being ambushed. I glared at Kip, whose expression remained neutral. I wanted to smack that mask of neutrality off his face.

"I wasn't fired," I said hotly. "I quit. And for the record, I don't get paid. I'm a volunteer. She can't fire me." Wasn't there an old saying that no good deed goes unpunished?

"Did you dislike her that much to quit after only one day?"

The anger bubbled over, and I snapped, "Yes, Officer. She was a horrible person. The equivalent of a rabid skunk. I couldn't work in this toxic environment. But I didn't kill her." My agitation moved to my hands as I waved them in the air. "Besides, if you were listening to anything at all I told you before, she and Commissioner Quackenbush were involved in illegal activities. Maybe you should be questioning him."

"We will, Dr. Reynolds, don't worry."

My adrenaline plummeted, and fatigue threatened to drag me under. "Look, I'm drained." I slumped back in my hard, uncomfortable chair. "Can I go home now?"

"Just a couple more questions," said Number Two. "Can you think of anyone else who might have wanted to harm Ms. Dilly?"

I snorted. "Boy, can I. I can think of several from yesterday alone. Who knows how many others there are? I imagine everyone who's ever come into contact with her would like to . . ." I'd almost said, "wring her neck." Thank goodness for filters. I reminded myself that one should speak kindly of the dead.

I told them about Gary, who should have had the director's job, but instead, was assigned to menial tasks—although I couldn't imagine Gary hurting a flea. Well, maybe a flea. But didn't he say that if she didn't back off, someone would have to pry his hands from her neck, or something like that? I didn't volunteer that information. No sense in the police seizing on an idle, thoughtless comment and making it into a threat of murder. But Gary's offhand comment embedded itself in my brain.

Then there was Marilee Meece, who'd had a run-in with Margot and became outraged at being called a stupid bimbo. As well she should. But again, I couldn't see the animal-loving philanthropist resorting to murder over name-calling. Now, Mr. Finkle was another story. But he'd gotten his dog back, and there were other ways to take Margot down besides strangling her. He'd as much as promised me he would go to the police instead of taking revenge. Now Stanley Quackenbush could be a prime suspect. He'd accused Margot of not bringing in enough money from the golf tournament, which—if one read between the lines—meant he suspected she'd skimmed more than her share. I believed him capable of anything. And how about his wife? Did Mrytle still think Stanley was cheating on her with Margot? Or did Margot calling her an old cow constitute a reason for murder?

Number One closed his notepad. "Okay, Dr. Reynolds, thanks for your time. We'll be in touch."

He and Number Two rose and headed back to the office, where the forensics team labored over the crime scene.

As soon as they had left the room, I unleashed my anger on Kip.

"Thanks a lot for telling them Margot fired me."

He held out his hands, as though fending off my attack. "I didn't."

Narrowing my eyes, I said, "Then how did they know? You were the only one I told."

Kip stuck his hand in his pocket and produced a folded piece of paper. "Office email."

"What?" My mouth hung open as I took the paper from him and read, "To all employees, I regret to inform you that Dr. Reynolds was fired for insubordination. We will be looking for a new veterinarian. In the meantime, you are to carry out your duties as usual. M. Dilly."

If Margot weren't already dead, I would have killed her. How dare she humiliate me in such a way? I clenched my jaw so tightly I was afraid I'd break a molar.

Another thought hit me hard enough to stop gritting my teeth over the humiliating and untrue email. "And just where were *you* while everything was going down? You were obviously in the building since you came running when I screamed. Didn't you hear anything before that, or did you have noise-cancelling earbuds in while listening to whale songs or a true-crime podcast called *How to Miss Obvious Murders?*" Robert Redford handsome or not, a badge didn't necessarily make someone a saint.

His lips flattened. "Margot made me leave after the shelter closed. She must have suspected I'd been in her office the night before." He let out a short, humorless laugh. "She told me it was bad enough to have to work with a parolee during the day, but she wasn't about to be alone with me in the building at night." Shaking his head, he said, "If only she really knew. If only I *had* been here."

I narrowed my eyes, not sure whether his story rang true or not. "So how come you were so conveniently here right after me?"

"I planned to swing back by after she left. She didn't know, of course, that I had a key." His shoulders drooped a fraction. "I went back to the station to catch up on some paperwork, then drove back, hoping she was gone. But I saw your car pull into the parking lot, and I wondered what you were up to. So, I waited for a few moments, then followed you in."

"You *what?*" Fresh anger tightened my gut. "What exactly did you *think* I was doing?"

He held both hands, palms up. "That's just it. I didn't know, but in my line of work, if something feels off, I have to check it out. Look, Amanda, I am not the bad guy here. I'm trying to get to the bottom of this mess."

Some of my anger diffused like air leaking out of a balloon. Kip was right. He wasn't the enemy. Then a new thought occurred to me. Now that I knew he wasn't a serial killer, perhaps I could take a rain check on that burger he'd offered last night. My stomach rumbled, reminding me that I hadn't had dinner. Spending a little one-on-one time with Kip might make up for the nightmare of this evening. Should I ask him?

"I'd better see what they've found so far," he said, breaking into my waffling thoughts. "Take care of yourself, Amanda."

With that, he was gone. I stood alone in the lobby, worried, depressed, and dog-tired. I picked up my purse and muttered, "Goodnight, Merlin."

"I love you," he replied.

Well, at least somebody did.

Chapter Nine

Despite my weariness, I couldn't sleep. My mind kept circling back to the past two days, chasing its own tail like a hyperactive terrier. Although I had no love for Margot, I never wanted to see the woman end up the way she did. What if I could have prevented the murder by walking into the shelter a few minutes earlier? Then again, I could've wound up as a chalk outline myself.

And the issue with the forged health certificates made my head swim. How many had Margot managed to put into the hands of unsuspecting pet adopters while I was away? And how would that reflect on me if one or more of those animals turned out to have a health problem? I knew who would be blamed, and the thing was, I might never even know about it. My professional reputation could be ruined by people telling other people about my incompetence—I knew how these stories about "bad" veterinarians snowballed. I felt my credentials hanging by a thin thread. "You know that vet can't tell the difference between a male and a female cat? Yeah, Amanda Reynolds, that's the one. Don't ever go to *her* clinic."

Could Barkley's Animal Clinic decide they didn't need the PR fiasco of an incompetent and maybe a criminal vet on staff? Much as I hated to air the shelter's dirty laundry, I had to let everyone at my paying job know what happened.

Another thought gnawed at me. What about the shelter animals? They were the real victims in all this mess. Who might Stanley Quackenbush appoint to take over for Margot? Did he have another shady crony waiting in the wings? A distant cousin with a diploma from the University of Craigslist? I had told the police about the dirty dealings between the commissioner and Margot, but what if Stanley could refute everything? After all, he was a politician—slicker than a greased pig at a county fair. He could deny everything and walk away smiling for the cameras.

Somehow, I had to convince the other commissioners to give the job to Gary. But what if Gary was the murderer? Could his skills as an administrator and his passion for animals outweigh the slight issue of eliminating evil people? After all, he had been pretty steamed at Margot.

Did I know any of the other commissioners? I racked my brain, but couldn't come up with any other names except for Natalie Tatum, picked more for her glossy smile than her grasp of public policy. Talking to her would be like talking to a decorative houseplant. She would stare at me through that wide-eyed, zero comprehension look of hers, indicating nothing was transferring into the one neuron in her cerebral cortex. The only reason I knew of Stanley and Mrytle Quackenbush was that they kept such a public profile—always in the news for this or that good deed. Always present for the photo ops.

Finally, there was the little matter of *me*. What if the police decided to bump me up on the suspect list? Margot and I'd argued. She'd embarrassed me by sending that email to all the shelter workers about my so-called "firing." Plus, I'd gone back to the shelter to confront her about forging my name. I could see where I might have a pretty plausible motive.

A chill crept over me, spreading to the tips of my fingers and toes. I didn't look good in orange either.

The expression, "looking like something the cat dragged in," might have been coined specifically for me when I hauled myself into work the next day. I'd spent a fitful night trying to get some rest while my brain decided that since I was just lying there, it was a good time to run through fifty-seven worst-case scenarios, none of which ended with me winning the lottery.

I wanted to break the news to my boss first, but he hadn't come in yet. Tiffany, on the other hand, had heard about Margot's death on the morning news.

"Amanda!" she cried, latching onto my arm like a leech. "Did you hear about the murder at the shelter last night?"

"I was there," I said, towing her along with me to the office so I could divest myself of my purse.

"What?" Her eyes rounded. "Oh my gosh! What happened?"

After closing the door, I began by telling her about the papers Margot had given Mrs. Huxley and how I had gone to confront Margot, but ended up finding her dead. Then I told her about Kip, the police, and how I might be a suspect.

Tiffany gasped so loudly I was sure the whole clinic heard. "A suspect? You? Amanda, you can barely kill a spider."

"True," I said. "But apparently yelling at Margot and being irate over her forging my name puts me in the running."

Tiffany clapped both hands over her mouth, then dropped them just as quickly. "Wait—did they take your fingerprints? Oh my gosh, did they swab you for DNA? Did they make you do the walk-of-shame in handcuffs?"

"Lower your voice," I muttered, not desiring to become the clinic's morning entertainment. "No handcuffs. No DNA swabs. Just a lot of repetitive questions until I thought about confessing to jaywalking, just to spice things up."

Tiffany's eyes gleamed, equal parts horror and delight. "This is *so* much better than true crime podcasts. Do you think they'll do a reenactment? Because if they do, I volunteer to play you."

I groaned. "Please, Tiffany. The only role you're getting in my murder investigation is 'nosy coworker number two.'"

Tiffany leaned in closer, whispering like we were plotting a jewel heist. "So, who do you think *really* did it?"

I opened my mouth to answer that I had no idea, but just then the office door swung open. Dr. Barkley strode in, coffee in one hand, car keys in the other.

"Who did what?" he asked cheerfully, like we were taking bets on the Kentucky Derby.

Tiffany nearly choked. "The *murder,* of course!"

Dr. Barkley froze mid-sip. His eyes ping-ponged between the two of us. "Excuse me?"

I threw up my hands. "She's talking about Margot Dilly. At the shelter. Last night."

"Oh, yes, I heard about that this morning." He clucked his tongue in that "such a tragedy, but it doesn't affect my full schedule" type of way.

I shot Tiffany a look to let me do the talking, but she didn't, of course. "And the police spent several hours last night grilling Amanda," she said, like she'd had a front row seat. "She might even be a suspect."

Dr. Barkley peered at me over his mug. "A suspect?"

I sighed. "Apparently, yelling at someone before they're murdered earns you a spot on the shortlist."

"So," he said slowly, lowering his coffee, "remind me not to argue with you about the thermostat settings again."

I managed a weak smile. "You always win anyway. You keep reminding me who pays the electric bill."

"Well, all I have to say is if the cops haul you away, you'd better have your surgeries finished first." He chuckled and walked out of the office.

"That went better than I expected," I said.

The busy morning managed to distract me from the train wreck that my life had become since returning to the States. At least it had the potential to. Tiffany kept circling back to the murder with the tenacity of a pit bull with a bone. I countered by pointing at charts, medications, and a rabbit under anesthesia, hoping she'd focus on something other than death and scandal. Just when I thought I had her contained, my phone buzzed.

Vanessa.

"Amanda! I just heard about Margot. Do you

know what happened?"

"Unfortunately, more than I'd like to. But I can't talk about it now. Can you meet me for lunch at Randolfs?"

"Sure. See you about noon?"

"That should work." I disconnected and got back to my rabbit spay, glad that Tiffany hadn't overheard. If she caught even a whiff of lunch plus murder talk, she'd have attached herself to me like a barnacle. Much as I liked her, she had a flair for drama, and I didn't need any more drama. I already had murder.

A few minutes after twelve, I slid into the back booth at Randolf's that Vanessa had already claimed. As quietly as possible, I related everything that had happened between the waitress interrupting us for our orders.

"Wow." She sat back, eyes wide, and took a sip of water. "Since this is my day off, I slept in late. I didn't hear about anything until I saw that Gary had tried to call me. The police have closed the shelter for a few days while they investigate."

"Is Gary going to be allowed to take care of the animals?"

"Yeah, the police are only letting him into the building. But he said they grilled him for two hours first."

I took a bite of my chicken salad. "What did they ask him?"

Vanessa paused mid-bite of her hamburger and

seemed to consider. "I can't really remember everything he told me," she said with her mouth full. She chewed and swallowed, thank goodness, before continuing. "How he felt when he wasn't hired as Frances' replacement. That kind of thing."

I hoped he hadn't told them about wanting to wrap his hands around Margot's neck. "What did he tell them?"

She shrugged. "Oh, just that he was disappointed, but he was a team player. That kind of thing."

I'd be willing to bet he left out the part about how angry he was over being delegated to grunt work. But it wasn't my place to stir the pot. Unless he was the killer.

"At least we can stop speculating about Kip's criminal record," I said. "Even though the tables have turned from *him* being a murderer to *me* being a murderer."

"Yeah, Gary told me. Imagine. Who would have thought he was working undercover?" Worry lines creased her face. "Amanda, what are you going to do? To take the focus off of you, I mean. You can't just sit around waiting for the police to clear you."

"I don't know." I sighed and laid down my fork, no longer hungry.

I could see the wheels turning in her mind as she nibbled on a French fry. "You know," she said thoughtfully, "I bet people would be more open in talking to us than the police. You know how people clam up with cops. But in a casual conversation with someone who's not investigating the case, somebody might let something slip."

I nearly choked on my Diet Coke. "Vanessa, are you seriously suggesting we play amateur detectives, like on *Murder She Wrote*?"

She shrugged. "Why not? We're all involved in this disaster. We know all the people. We can ask questions without looking suspicious. You know, talk to people in a non-threatening way, just like we're doing now."

I shook my head. "I don't know. We're veterinary professionals. We don't know anything about police investigations."

"Exactly my point. No one will suspect us of ulterior motives."

"But it could be dangerous. You do realize we could be putting ourselves directly in the path of a murderer?" A shudder ran up my spine. The image of Margot's lifeless face flashed through my mind.

"It wouldn't be dangerous if they don't catch on to what we're really doing. We'd just be talking." Her eyes shone with excitement as she dabbed another French fry into her ketchup.

"Van, you're not a suspect. Why would you want to endanger yourself trying to help me?"

She shrugged again. "I don't know. Maybe because this is the most exciting thing to happen in this town since the night someone spray-painted a mustache on the poster of the mayor's face during Founder's

Day."

"Vanessa, this is not a game!" I hissed.

Her expression turned to steely determination. "I'm well aware of that. But let's face it. The police in this town haven't had any crimes of this magnitude in—" she waved her hands—"I don't know if they've ever had a crime of this magnitude. I think Mr. Corbet's shooting a rifle into the air to scare Farmer Murphy's cow off his property constitutes the worst crime the police have ever dealt with. They don't exactly have the NYPD's experience. If we want answers, Amanda, maybe it's up to us."

I mulled over her words, which, in some twisted way, seemed to make some sense. "But where would we even start?"

A sly grin lifted the corners of her mouth. "Leave it to me."

Against all better judgment, I reluctantly agreed.

Back at work, I shoved the whole, unreal conversation to the back of my mind where I hoped it would shrivel up and die. Surely, once Vanessa had time to reflect on the wisdom of her plan, she would come to her senses.

No such luck. At four o'clock, she called to say she was picking me up after work to visit Mr. Finkle to "check on Percy." I was in way over my head and about to embark on swimming with sharks.

Chapter Ten

Vanessa insisted on swinging through a fast-food joint on the way to Mr. Finkle's house. She ordered a large combo meal—supersized, naturally, because apparently murder investigations require the stamina of a lumberjack. The thought of grease made my stomach churn, so I settled for a Diet Coke.

She drove with one hand loosely on the steering wheel, the other buried elbow-deep into the bag like it was a gold mine. The paper rustled with the enthusiasm of a raccoon in a dumpster.

"Here, let me help you with that before you kill us," I said. I snatched the bag out of her hand, fished out her sandwich, unwrapped it, and passed it to her. "We can't solve a murder if you kill us by running us into a telephone pole while wrestling a chicken sandwich."

"So, here's the plan," she said around a mouthful of crispy chicken, her words muffled and punctuated with lettuce crunch. "We'll say we're from the shelter—which we are—and how sorry we are about what happened to Percy. Which we are. We're just checking to make sure he's okay. No PTSD from his dognapping experience."

"He didn't appear to be overly traumatized to me," I said. "Mrs. Huxley seemed like a nice lady."

"That's not the point," Vanessa said, her exasperation launching crumbs across the dashboard like confetti. "It's our excuse to get our foot in the door. Amanda, you've got to stop thinking so literally and start thinking like a sleuth."

I sighed. "I don't think I'm cut out for all this subterfuge. I'm basically a truthful person. I sing in the church choir, which is tricky if I'm lying through my teeth on Saturday and belting out hymns on Sunday."

She shot me an annoyed look. "Amanda, there's lying for nefarious purposes, and then there's lying for a good cause. There *is* a difference."

I wasn't sure I could see the difference, but I kept this thought to myself.

"Just let me do the talking."

"That's what scares me," I muttered.

We pulled up to Mr. Finkle's house, a low-slung ranch with peeling shutters and a roof that had seen better days. The front yard was small but tidy, a patch of grass hemmed in by a cracked concrete sidewalk and a mailbox leaning at a permanent angle, as if it had given up on life. A faded plastic flamingo stood guard near the front steps, its pink long ago bleached to a dull peach by the sun.

The neighborhood itself was pure middle-class suburbia, the kind of place where houses wore their sameness like a uniform—one-story brick or clapboard homes lined neatly in a row, each with a driveway just wide enough for a sedan and maybe a rusty pickup. Kids' bicycles were abandoned in a couple of yards, their wheels spinning in the faint breeze, and the soft thump of a basketball echoed from somewhere down the street. A woman in yoga pants jogged past with a golden retriever that gave our car a perfunctory sniff before moving on.

My pulse kicked up at the idea of seeing the large man again. Vanessa was already halfway up to the door while I sat in the passenger seat, trying to summon my courage.

She turned. "You coming?"

I sucked in a fortifying breath, which did nothing to calm my shaky nerves, and got out. With any luck, maybe Mr. Finkle wouldn't be home.

Vanessa jabbed the doorbell, and from inside the house, we heard Percy singing the song of his people. A moment later, the door swung open, and Jerome Finkle's bulky frame filled the doorway. Percy pressed happily against his leg like a furry security system.

A flicker of confusion crossed Mr. Finkle's face. "Can I help you?"

"Hi, Mr. Finkle, I'm Vanessa from the animal shelter, and you remember Dr. Reynolds." She nodded to me.

"Oh, yes, of course." His jowly face broke into a smile, and he stepped back to admit us. "I can't tell you how grateful I am to you for finding Percy. Come in, come in."

He ushered us into a living room that looked like it had been decorated sometime in the late seventies and then carefully preserved ever since. The carpet was a faded avocado green, flattened in the middle where countless footsteps had worn a path from the door to the couch. The couch itself sagged in the middle, as if it had given up years ago, its floral upholstery dulled to muted browns and oranges. A walnut-veneer coffee table sat in front of it, its surface scarred with ring marks from decades of sweating glasses.

The walls told their own story. Above the fireplace hung a taxidermized bass, its glassy eyes staring blankly across the room. Framed sports posters lined one wall—local teams mostly, their colors faded and edges curling, as though they'd endured too many summers without air conditioning. Wedged between them were family photographs, school portraits spanning decades of questionable hairstyles, and a framed, yellowed newspaper clipping boasting of a high-school championship long past.

The room smelled faintly of dust and old upholstery, with just a hint of pipe tobacco, as if the walls themselves had soaked it in. The whole room gave off the impression of someone who had lived here a long time and wasn't planning to change a thing. I knew, instinctively, that no Mrs. Finkle resided here.

"Sit down," he said, waving us to the sofa. "Would you like something to drink? Beer? A glass of water?"

"No, thank you," I murmured, shuddering to imagine what his clean glasses might look like under a blacklight.

He sank into the La-Z-Boy opposite us with a grunt and leaned forward, his hands dangling between his knees. "Well, this is a nice surprise. What can I do for you ladies?"

"Well, actually, it's what we can do for *you*, Mr. Finkle," said Vanessa, her voice dripping with sincerity. "We are *so* sorry about what happened with Percy, and just wanted to make sure he was okay after his awful ordeal."

I held in my snort. Yeah, life with Mrs. Huxley had been unspeakable.

The man placed a fond hand on the neck of his dog. "That's very kind of you, but Percy's just fine. He's a resilient fellow." The collie returned the look with canine devotion.

Vanessa pressed on. "And we wanted to assure you that the shelter would never condone what Margot Dilly did. She acted completely on her own."

Well, Margot and Stanley Quackenbush. But I held my tongue.

Jerome Finkle's face darkened. "I know. I filed a police complaint yesterday. I hope that woman not only gets fired but goes to jail."

I studied him carefully. Did he truly not know she was dead? Or was he merely a good actor?

Vanessa's countenance turned somber. "So, I take it you haven't heard."

His eyes bounced back and forth between us. "Heard what?"

"Margot Dilly was found murdered last night."

Mr. Finkle's eyes widened. He blew out a long breath and ran a hand through his thinning hair. "No. What happened?"

I had to admit, the man looked genuinely shocked.

Vanessa lowered her voice. "Someone came into the shelter and killed her."

He shook his head. I waited to see if he would accidentally slip and blurt out something about strangulation and leashes, but nothing came out.

"Oh, man." Mr. Finkle appeared genuinely shaken. He blinked several times, absently stroking the dog at his side. Finally, he swallowed and said, "Well, I can't say I wasn't plenty upset by what she did. But murder . . ."

I spoke for the first time. "Mr. Finkle, the police may want to talk to you since you had a grievance against Margot."

He slumped back into his chair. "Oh." After several silent seconds, he said, "I guess it looks bad for me." His gaze met mine. "But I didn't kill her. I swear. I bluster a lot, but I couldn't hurt anyone."

"I know," I said, although I couldn't say for certain I knew. Still, something about the big man made me believe him.

"Well," said Vanessa, as she stood, "we didn't mean to upset you. We primarily wanted to check on Percy and express the shelter's deep regret over what happened. Until Margot took over, the shelter was above reproach."

His eyes glazed. "She was an evil woman, but nobody deserves to be murdered."

"Thank you for your time, Mr. Finkle," I said, moving swiftly to the door.

He didn't get up to see us out.

Back in the car, I risked one more glance at the house. Vanessa started the engine, and we pulled away.

"So, what's your take on him?" I asked as I fastened my seat belt.

"I don't think he did it. He seemed to be completely blindsided by the news." She came to a stop at the stop sign at the end of the street.

"I agree. I'm inclined to believe him." I stared out the window as the cookie-cutter houses blurred by. "So now what?"

She grinned. "We move on to suspect number two."

"Which is?"

"I haven't gotten that far yet. There's Mrs. Meece, Mr. and Mrs. Quackenbush, and Gary—although I can't imagine he would kill anybody."

"That's because you're prejudiced in his favor." For that matter, so was I.

"True," she admitted. She tapped the wheel, thoughtful.

"Besides, for all we know, it could be a hundred other people who had a reason to want Margot dead. Did you see anyone else argue with her? You were there for three weeks before I got back."

She nibbled on her lower lip. "Not that I can think of. But, then again, she kept me busy with scut work behind the scenes."

I blew out a breath. "It could even be someone not associated with the shelter. Surely, with her sparkling personality, she made enemies outside of work."

"Yeah, but the timing is too coincidental. The murder took place right after she had serious altercations with several people."

"But can you honestly see any of the others you mentioned as a murderer?"

"Commissioner Quackenbush? Absolutely!" Vanessa gripped the steering wheel harder. "Perhaps he should be next on our list."

I shivered. "Couldn't we start with someone less likely murder-y? Like Mrs. Meece?"

"Fine." Vanessa appeared deep in thought, then brightened. "I've got the perfect idea to get her to see us."

"What?"

"The shelter owes her a huge apology for the way she was treated. Plus—" Vanessa shot me a conspiratorial look—"the shelter needs her money."

"Van, that's—"

"I know, I know. But it's true." She smiled in the same way a cat looks after deliberately knocking something off a shelf—slow, satisfied, and utterly unapologetic. "We'll flatter her, acknowledge and apologize for her grievances, and sprinkle enough guilt to get her attention. It's foolproof."

I couldn't help but laugh. "Foolproof, huh? Then we've got the right team."

"I'll handle the theatrics. You are the innocent sidekick, which fits you perfectly. Relax, this is going to be fun."

I stared at her. Fun? Really? How had my life suddenly become an amateur criminal investigation with a side of fast food and bad decisions? I was definitely going to need more than a Diet Coke to survive this.

Chapter Eleven

The events of the past few days had taken their toll. I looked like the "before" photo in a makeover ad. Tiffany pounced on me the next morning like a squirrel on an acorn.

"You look terrible! Where did you go last night?"

"Uh, gee, thanks." It dawned on me too late that Vanessa had picked me up from the clinic in her car, leaving mine to cool its heels in the parking lot way past closing time. Naturally, Tiffany had noticed. Thinking fast, I said, "Oh, I just had dinner with a friend." Which was technically true. Vanessa had eaten dinner, and she was my friend. "We got back late, that's all."

Tiffany's eyes narrowed. "Is there a new man in your life?" Immediately, her face lit up like someone had just told her there was cake in the break room. "Who is he? You have to tell me everything."

I brushed past her on my way to the office. "There is no 'he.'" I sighed. Tiffany would find out sooner or later. "It was Vanessa, okay?"

Tiffany's expression crumpled. She'd always had a prick of jealousy toward Vanessa for reasons that I never could fathom. "Oh." Her voice took on a wounded tone.

I set my purse on my desk, pushed Oscar aside, and booted up my computer. "Tiff, it was shelter business. Otherwise, we would have invited you along."

"Shelter business?" Her attention snapped back into true crime mode faster than a TV remote. "You mean the murder?"

Not trusting myself to meet her eyes—I was a bad liar, which I guess came from my strong Baptist upbringing—I hesitated. "Well, of course, the murder is on everyone's mind."

She parked on the edge of my desk. "Are there any suspects? Besides you, I mean."

"I really don't know." I busied myself with call-back reminders as though that would make her take the hint and back off. When she didn't, I said, "Could you go see if our first appointment is here? If not, I need to start returning some calls."

Tiffany gave me a rather annoyed look before sauntering out of the office.

The hearty voice of Dr. Barkley greeted me from the doorway. "Oh, good! I see you're not in jail." He chuckled, dropped his keys on his desk, and took a slurp of his coffee.

I fought down a sarcastic retort. I didn't see anything funny about my situation. Or the situation as a whole, for that matter. A woman had been murdered.

He must have picked up on my lack of amusement. "Sorry, Amanda. I know this whole thing is upsetting for you."

I rubbed my throbbing temples. "You can say that again. I mean, if you can't feel safe in a building full of dogs and cats, where can you?"

He gave me a sympathetic look. "Well, from what I've heard, Margot Dilly was universally disliked. I think the murder had more to do with the person than the environment."

"True, but I'm not sure I can ever walk in there again without . . . you know." I glanced at the callback charts on my desk, but my mind lingered on the scene in the shelter office.

Dr. Barkley gave me an awkward pat on the back. "Well, if there's anything you need—time off, someone to cover your shelter day, bail money—just let me know." He strode from the office before I could remind him that I'd quit my shelter job, and the reference to bail money wasn't helpful.

Tiffany burst in, nearly colliding with Dr. Barkley and his ever-present cup of coffee. "Amanda, there's a *police officer* here to see you!"

My heart did a flip until she added, "And what a hunk! I hope he posed for the police calendar."

Kip. Hopefully, he wasn't here to arrest me.

Swallowing down the panic that had crawled into my throat at the words "police officer," I said, "Show him in."

Tiffany disappeared and hustled back, leading Kip as though she was escorting royalty. She leaned over and whispered into my ear, "He can handcuff me anytime," before making her exit and closing the door.

My face burned with her totally inappropriate comment, and I turned away and cleared my throat. "Officer Gallagher," I said, my back still toward him as I willed my heated face to cool. "What can I do for you?" I swiveled slightly to meet his eye, unable to shake the mental image Tiffany had conjured up.

"Kip. Call me Kip." He smiled like a man who rehearsed casual charm in front of a mirror.

I nodded and gestured toward Dr. Barkley's unoccupied chair. "Please, have a seat."

Kip sat with the practiced ease of a man comfortable in his own skin. I felt my eyes drift to his left hand, which I hadn't taken notice of before. No ring. No tan line.

Oscar abandoned my desk and jumped into Kip's vacant lap, where he could shed liberally all over Kip's uniform.

"Amanda, I called Mr. Finkle this morning to set up a meeting. He told me that you and Vanessa had been to his house last night." Kip's gorgeous blue eyes drilled into me.

Wow. The man was really good at his job. I tried to adopt an air of nonchalance, but I worried that my poor lying skills would be quickly exposed.

I diverted my eyes away from his prying gaze. Shoot, I couldn't remember if liars usually looked to the left or the right. I'd seen that information posted somewhere on social media, but couldn't pull the memory from my brain.

"Uh, yes, we were," I said. "We wanted to make sure his dog, Percy, was okay after Margot had dognapped him and sold him to someone else."

I could still feel the intense heat of Kip's eyes on me. "Uh, huh." His tone said he wasn't buying my excuse. "He told me you'd also informed him about Margot's murder."

Casting a quick peek in Kip's direction, I bumped up against that intense gaze again.

"I wish you hadn't done that," he said. "Now I can't catch him off guard with the news and gauge his reaction."

Oh. I hadn't thought about the surprise factor. "We didn't mean to create problems with the investigation," I lied. "We just wanted to check on Percy's welfare." I risked locking eyes with Kip. "Animal welfare is our job, after all." I tried to make my reason for visiting Mr. Finkle sound official and not like Vanessa and I had been gossiping in his living room. Or trying to figure out if he might be a murderer.

Kip blew out a long breath through pinched lips that suggested both controlled patience and exasperation. "I suppose no major harm was done. Still, I'm going to have to ask you to stay away from anyone who's a potential suspect. You could impede our investigation as well as potentially put yourself in danger."

"If it's any help, both Vanessa and I got the impression that Mr. Finkle was truly shocked by the news of Margot's death. We don't think he did it."

Kip's jaw tightened, and I knew I'd blabbed the wrong thing. "Dr. Reynolds," he began.

Uh-oh. We were back to formalities, which meant he'd had enough and was switching into full-procedural mode.

"You are not a trained law-enforcement officer. You don't have the expertise to judge when a suspect is lying." He got to his feet, dumping Oscar onto the floor in the process, and brushed cat hair from his uniform. Oscar gave him a wounded look and hopped back up on my desk. "Please, for everyone's sake, stick to neutering cats and dogs and leave the police work to the police."

The sting of his rebuke hit hard, and indignity burned in my chest. I wasn't just a neutering machine. But now was not the time to enlighten him. I supposed the opportunity of grabbing a burger with Officer

Redford, er, Gallagher, had gone with the wind. Now, he not only viewed me as an unwanted extra burden to his job, but he also considered *my* job trivial.

Unable to trust myself to speak, I simply nodded.

"Take care, Dr. Reynolds. And stay safe." With those parting words, Kip left me sitting in my seat of shame.

No sooner had the door clicked shut than Tiffany swooped back in like a cat zeroing in on a laser dot.

"Well, what did he want? Did he ask you out?"

I pinned her with my most no-nonsense stare. "No, he didn't ask me out. We are *not* dating." Darn it. Although my involvement in his ongoing investigation might make a relationship awkward.

"Then can I ask *him* out? Did you get his number?"

"Tiffany! Have some self-respect. Don't go throwing yourself at a handsome face." I shuffled my stack of callbacks, none of which I'd gotten to, to indicate the conversation was over.

"It's better than throwing myself at an ugly face," she replied. "Anyway, you've got a client waiting. And she's pretty upset."

Swell. Just what I needed. Heaving myself out of my chair, I walked slowly to the exam room. Could this day—that had only just begun—possibly get any worse? I quickly relayed to my brain that it was a rhetorical question, not a challenge.

I opened the door to exam room one to find a sour-looking older woman clutching a handful of papers as though they were evidence in a crime. With the way my past few days had been going, maybe they were. And no animal. Oh, no. These were the worst. Without an animal to soften the mood of the client, I was on my own.

"Hello," I greeted, holding out my hand and forcing a smile. "I'm Dr. Reynolds. What can I do for you today?"

The woman shoved the papers into my outstretched hand. "You can explain to me why you allowed a dog with a heart condition to be adopted out of the shelter as 'healthy.'"

Confused, I separated the papers and laid them on the exam table. The top one was the medical record from a colleague. I scanned the physical findings. Under the exam, the vet had noted a grade 4/6 holosystolic murmur. Flipping to the next page, I read the radiology report. The dog had an enlarged heart with a vertebral heart score of 13 (well above the normal 10.5 average) and mild interstitial changes in the lungs. Lab work showed an elevated troponin, suggestive of heart disease. Besides the heart issues, the dog had a significant amount of dental tartar, an ear infection, and bilateral grade 3 patellar luxation. The dog's age was estimated at about ten years.

Thankfully, the lady remained quiet while I perused the records. Then I turned to the shelter intake form, and anger bubbled up in my stomach. The intake form listed the dog's age as two, and all the systems were checked off as normal. At the bottom was my signature—which was a poor forgery—and dated for a day when I'd been snorkeling in Belize.

I looked at the name on the adoption paperwork. Looking up, I said, "I'm sorry to tell you this, Mrs. Briggs, but this isn't my signature."

"What do you mean, this isn't your signature?" The lady drew herself up for a good tongue-lashing. "It has your name right there." She stabbed at the name with a thick finger as proof.

"Yes, ma'am, but you see, I was out of the country that day. Someone forged my name."

Confusion wrinkled her brow. "Forged?"

There was no easy way to soften the ugly truth. "Yes. I'm afraid the new manager took it upon herself to illegally practice veterinary medicine in my absence. She forged my name on the health records in order to move animals out of the shelter quickly."

Mrs. Briggs' face turned the color of an overripe tomato. "What?" She sputtered to find the right words for the situation. "Why, that is unconscionable! I'm going to report her and demand my money back for Winston."

"I completely sympathize, but I'm afraid reporting her won't do any good at this point. She died two days ago."

Now the color in Mrs. Briggs' face drained to a sallow shade of gray. "Died?" She seemed to consider the news carefully.

"I'm very sorry you were deceived. I'm sure the shelter will take Winston back and refund your money."

"Take him back?" She looked at me like I had two heads. "I don't want to give him back. I searched for two months for a young adult pug, and the lady at the shelter called me two days later with Winston. I'm already attached to him. And he's attached to me."

"That's very kind of you, but because of the director's misrepresentation, you've ended up with an old dog with health problems who will no doubt require a lot of veterinary care."

"It doesn't matter. Maybe Winston was meant to be mine. Sometimes we older folk need more love." A single tear trickled out of the corner of her eye.

My heart did a soft, warm flutter. Until she added, "But it's a good thing that woman's dead. Otherwise, I'd *kill* her."

I flinched and ended the appointment as quickly as possible. I made a mental note to call my colleague who'd examined Winston and tell her I really wasn't as incompetent as the shelter paperwork made me out to be. Thank goodness, I'd managed to pacify one rightfully angry adoptive pet parent. But how many more fraudulent records were out there?

Chapter Twelve

Vanessa called right as I was halfway through a tuna sandwich and trying to return phone calls with my mouth full.

"I've been trying to reach Mrs. Meece," she said. "So far, no luck."

"That may be for the best," I said, brushing crumbs off my keyboard. "Between Kip officially telling me to back off the investigation and Tiffany's hurt feelings that she wasn't included in our adventure last night, maybe we should drop all this sleuthing nonsense."

"Drop it?" Vanessa's voice rose an octave. "Amanda, we can't drop it. As shelter employees, we're in the perfect position to talk to people. The murderer may let down their guard around us and say something they would never say to the police."

I had to admit she had a point. "But what do we tell Kip?"

"We don't need to tell him anything. We have a right to talk to people who have a connection to the shelter."

Sure, it sounded so logical when *she* said it. "What about the danger we might be putting ourselves in?"

"Nobody is going to suspect us doing anything other than gossiping about the biggest news to hit the shelter since someone left the de-scented skunk on the doorstep. I don't think even the new paint job completely got rid of that smell. Anyway, why would anyone think we have ulterior motives?"

Logical again. "Okay," I said. "Besides, someone really does owe Mrs. Meece an apology."

I could almost hear her grin through the phone. "Great! I'll keep trying to reach Mrs. Meece, and I'll pick you up after work."

"Wait." I swallowed my last bite of tuna. "If Tiffany sees my car in the parking lot again, she'll blow this up into a full-blown soap opera, complete with a one-woman inquisition. I'll drive home and feed Eleanor, who, by the way, was rather put out with me last night for serving her dinner late. She sat on my pillow and glared at me until sunrise."

An audible huff sounded in the receiver. "You and that spoiled cat. Fine. I'll pick you up at six-thirty."

I would have offered to drive, but Vanessa's nerves were steadier than mine. "All right. See you then."

At six-thirty, Vanessa appeared at my door, perky and ready to roll. I had spent extra time with my sulky kitty and fed her her favorite canned food—mixed grill—so hopefully Eleanor would forgive me for abandoning her yet again this evening.

"I still couldn't reach Mrs. Meece, but I saw Gary's car in the parking lot at the shelter. Let's pick up some fast food and swing by to chat with our old friend."

I picked up my purse as a thought occurred to me. "Vanessa, why would you suspect Gary, but not me?"

She shrugged. "Maybe because he got such a raw deal. Maybe because Margot treated him like a human doormat. Maybe because he literally said something about wrapping his hands around Margot's neck. Maybe because he has red hair."

I rolled my eyes. "What does red hair have to do with anything?"

"Nothing. But it couldn't be you. You can't even step on a cockroach."

She had me there. I couldn't stand the crunch of their little exoskeletons. "No, but I can and will *spray* them," I said. "From a distance."

"Exactly my point. I can't see you getting close enough to Margot to slip a leash around her neck, let alone having the strength to subdue her by choking her.

She'd slip those talons out and saw her way through the nylon in a flash." Vanessa mimed tiny, vicious scissors with her fingers.

Regardless of her reasoning, I was glad Vanessa had my back. I *did* find Margot's body, after all, which made me a prime suspect, whether I liked it or not.

"All right. Let's go see Gary."

We swung through a hot-and-ready pizza place and grabbed an extra-large pepperoni and sodas. Although this wasn't my favorite pizza joint, I didn't much care about the cuisine. Again, my stomach twisted in knots, even though we were only going to talk to Gary. After all, my brain pointed out, how many times did you think you knew somebody only to find out they were a serial killer? Well, in my case, none. But I watched *Dateline*.

We crept into the shelter's back parking lot like the pair of amateur sleuths we were, and parked in the shadows. We didn't want Kip or any other nosy police officers, who had specifically declared the building off-limits to everyone but Gary, to see the car. Vanessa used her key to let us in.

"Hello," she called out as we stepped inside. "We come bearing pizza."

Gary appeared around the corner, a smile lighting up his tired face. "Hey, guys. What're you doing here?"

"We saw your car and thought we'd stop in." She changed her tone to sympathetic. "So, how's everything going?"

He ran a hand through his perpetually disheveled hair and heaved a sigh. "It's a mess. Come on back."

Merlin's head popped up out of his feed bowl as we walked past. He let out a loud wolf whistle, followed by, "Hello, beautiful."

I stopped to scratch his head. "Hello, Merlin. How's my favorite feathered friend?"

"This place is a mess," he shrieked. I withdrew my hand with a loud sigh.

"I think I already mentioned that," Gary quipped with a wry smile.

We followed Gary into the office, where an avalanche of paperwork littered the desktop. He shoved a pile aside to make room for the pizza box, which released a small, comforting steam of cheese that felt like a temporary truce with the world. A shudder rattled me. This room evoked visions of the last time I was in this office. With a very dead Margot. I started to suggest we eat and talk in the break room, but Gary had already opened the box and was halfway through his first slice of pizza.

"Mmm," he mumbled around a mouthful of marinara sauce and cheese. "This is just what I needed. Thanks."

I settled into one of the seats across from what had been Margot's throne and later her death chair and tried not to think about her dead body.

Vanessa perched beside me and reached for a few of the folders on top. "What is all this stuff?"

Gary chewed and swallowed. "That's what I'm trying to decipher. Margot had three different sets of books. One for the shelter, one for Stanley Quackenbush, and one for herself. It's impressive, in a horrifying sociopathic way, how much damage and deception she managed to pull off in less than a month."

"You do know about her arrangement with Stanley Quackenbush?" I phrased my statement in the form of a question.

He nodded as he bit into another slice. "Probably not the whole extent. But from her accounting, I can see where the two of them siphoned off funds. And as if that isn't complicated enough, she had a third set of books that clearly show she was holding out on Stanley."

Gary had just confirmed Commissioner Quackenbush's and my suspicions, shoving him way to the top of the list of suspects. Being cheated out of ill-gotten money from your thieving partner was a powerful motive for murder. I guess the saying, "There is no honor among thieves," really was true.

"I still can't believe she was actually stealing and selling purebred dogs." Gary uncapped a bottle of Mountain Dew and took a long drink. "Not to mention what she stole from the golf tournament."

"I wonder how long she would have gotten away with her actions if . . ." I left my sentence unfinished.

Regardless of how horrible a person Margot was, nobody deserved what had happened to her.

"Can you believe she even sold Merlin?"

"What?" Vanessa and I squawked together. We exchanged horrified looks.

"No way," I said, recovering from my shock. "She sold our shelter mascot?"

Gary nodded. "I got a call from a lady claiming she paid Margot one thousand dollars for Merlin, but she never delivered him."

I flashed back to that awful night—the silence when I'd yelled at Margot, the horror of discovering she was dead, and Merlin perched in a carrier, unusually quiet. I'd wondered why he was there. Now I knew.

A shadow crossed Gary's face. "Selling Merlin in and of itself is a good enough reason to kill Margot. If she weren't already dead."

Vanessa's mouth still hung open. She finally seemed to realize it and closed it. "So, now what? We can't give her Merlin."

Gary drew in a long breath. "No, of course not. The shelter will just have to come up with a thousand dollars to refund the money. No telling what Margot did with it. I can't find an extra thousand dollars in any of the books, including the cooked ones."

"Wow. That's a lot of money. Will the shelter be able to cover that?" I asked.

He rubbed his temples. "I've got to talk to our board of directors. Hopefully, they can figure something out, because right now, as you can well imagine, donations are dead in the water and we're barely keeping the lights on." A look of utter defeat came over his face, and his shoulders slumped with the weight of the shelter—and Margot's mess—pulling him down.

I resisted the sudden urge to giggle at Gary's unintended pun of "dead in the water."

"Well," Vanessa said brightly, changing the subject, "at least you are the director, as you rightfully should have been all along."

Despite his "promotion," Gary didn't look all that pleased. "For now. I don't know how I'm ever going to sort through all this. Plus, the shelter's reputation is likely to take a significant hit once word of what happened here spreads. No one will trust us with donations again. I'm not even sure the county will want to continue funding us."

"I hope Stanley Quackenbush is thrown in jail," Vanessa said, vehemence in her tone.

"He's a politician. He's used to lying his way out of sticky situations," Gary said. "It will be his word against a dead woman's."

"But I overheard their conversation," I said. "I specifically heard them talking about the money raised at the golf tournament."

They both stared at me like I held a live grenade. "You didn't tell me that," said Vanessa. "That makes you a witness." Her eyes grew wide. "Does Quackenbush know you heard them?"

My extremities went numb with the realization that I had told the police about Margot and Stanley's nefarious activities. If Stanley knew I could testify against him, would he try to kill me, too? Did he do his own dirty work or send a hitman? Suddenly, I felt the need to acquire a Rottweiler.

I shook my head. "But I told the police." Surely, they would protect me, their only material witness, right? Kip's warning sounded in my ears.

Vanessa shook her head. "You know what's really creepy? Just the day before Margot was killed, you said someone would have to pry your hands from her neck. Crazy, right?" She locked eyes with Gary.

I watched the expression on Gary's face flicker from surprise to anger to hurt.

Finally, he frowned. "I hope you're not insinuating that I killed her."

Vanessa held up her hand, palm outward. "Oh, no, of course not. It's just creepy weird, like I said."

"I was just blowing off steam. Sure, I was upset to be passed over for Frances' job and then treated like Margot's personal errand boy. But gee whiz, Van, I could never kill anyone." His lip quivered as though he might cry. "You know me better than that."

Vanessa huffed out a weak laugh. "Oh, Gary, I didn't mean anything."

He looked unconvinced. "I had even started scoping out other jobs."

"I think this murder has unnerved all of us," I said. The more I studied Gary's stricken face, the more I felt he couldn't have done it. "Have the police indicated when you may be able to reopen the shelter?"

He pulled his eyes away from Vanessa, a slice of pizza with a single bite out of it still in his hand. "No. And I don't know where things will stand when we do reopen."

Uh-oh. I hoped Vanessa hadn't burned her bridges with her job. As for me, I didn't know where I stood, either. Technically, I'd quit. But that was when Margot was still in charge. I would be willing to come back for Gary. That was, unless he really *did* murder Margot. The pizza sat between us, growing less appetizing by the minute.

I needed to get out of here. My thoughts scrambled in my brain to the point where I didn't trust my own judgment.

"Is there anything we can do to help?" I asked, changing the subject. "Clean cages, feed animals?"

He shook his head. "No, but thank you." He set down his uneaten piece of pizza on the cluttered desk. "And thanks for the pizza. But I'd better get back to work."

Vanessa and I exchanged glances and took the hint. Rising, she said, "Okay. If you need anything, call." We left the pizza and walked out.

"Stupid bimbo!" Merlin called as we passed his cage. Gary followed, closing and locking the back door behind us.

"Rats," she said, opening her door and slipping into the driver's seat. "I really hurt his feelings. And I thought I was being subtle."

I snorted. "Subtlety is not your strong suit, Van."

She turned to face me as I fastened my seat belt. "Well, how else was I supposed to bring up what he'd said about strangling Margot? It was pretty self-incriminating, don't you think? Plus, he just said in there that selling Merlin was justification for murdering her."

"Oh, I don't know. We all say things when we're angry that we don't mean literally."

We sat for a moment, each of us lost in our own thoughts.

She started the engine and backed out of the parking space. "I'm not sure we can cross Gary off our list of suspects. Although I feel bad for even considering him."

"You're right. Just because he's our friend doesn't mean we shouldn't be objective. He did have a good motive." My stomach rumbled, reminding me that I hadn't eaten even one slice of pizza.

Vanessa laughed. "I didn't have any pizza, either. Want to stop by the Golden Arches on the way home?"

"Sure. If Stanley Quackenbush doesn't kill me next, the fast food might." I sighed. "I admit, on further reflection, that I'm a little reluctant to approach him."

"At least alone," she agreed. Then that expression came over her face that I had come to dread. She was conjuring up another whacky idea. "But the council meeting is coming up. Maybe we can ambush him and question him there."

"I doubt he's going to admit anything in front of a roomful of people. Especially to us."

"He doesn't know who we are. Maybe we can pretend to be reporters." Her expression grew crazier. "We can wear disguises and give fake names."

I closed my eyes and leaned my head back against the seat. "Van, you can't be serious."

"Why not?"

"Because it's . . . it's—"

"Perfect!" she said.

Chapter Thirteen

To my surprise—and delight—Kip called the next day to invite me for coffee after work. I prayed it was for social, not interrogative, reasons. The anticipation buoyed me through the packed morning of barking dogs, hissing cats, and one owner who insisted her iguana needed a therapy session for depression.

Tiffany, mercifully, stayed too busy to grill me on updates at the shelter and ferret out my after-hours detective work.

My good mood lasted until after lunch, when I returned to find a mysterious cardboard box on my desk. As I moved closer, a noise emanating from the box startled me. Tiffany sidled into the office, a knowing smirk on her face.

"Open it," she said.

I eyed the box as it gave a faint wobble. "Is there something in there that might jump out and attack me?"

"Probably not."

Her unhelpful answer made my pulse kick up. I took a cautious step forward, the box now rustling ominously.

"Define 'probably.'"

"Just open it already."

Curiosity won out over sound judgment. I approached the box and lifted the lid. Four very young, fluffy kittens stared back at me. With the light suddenly streaming into their dark environment, they all blinked at me, then erupted into meows loud enough to raise the dead.

"Okay, they're adorable," I admitted. "But where did they come from, and why are they on my desk?"

Tiffany plopped herself into Dr. Barkley's seat like she was settling in for story hour. Clearly, she wanted to drag out the suspense for as long as possible. "A lady dropped them off while you were at lunch."

Not knowing where this revelation was heading, but already not liking what I was hearing, I said, "What do you mean by 'dropped them off?' This isn't an animal shelter. Call her back and tell her to come get them."

"She said they were for you." Tiffany was enjoying herself way too much.

"Me?" I pointed at my chest. "Why me? I didn't order any kittens."

She crossed her arms over her chest, drawing out the tension. "It's a long story."

I was in no mood for Tiffany's theatrics. "Just give me the summary."

Tiffany heaved a sigh for effect. "It seems this woman adopted a fat, fluffy neutered male cat from the shelter a few weeks ago."

I closed my eyes and pinched the bridge of my nose. "Let me guess—"

"She named him Tom, a rather unimaginative name for a male cat, if you ask me. And two days later, Tom had kittens." Tiffany had no intention of relinquishing the story, although I had pretty much figured out the ending. "It turns out that Tom is actually Tomasina."

"So it would appear," I said, dryly.

"The lady was not happy. She tried calling the shelter, but Margot refused to take her calls. So she Googled 'kitten care' and learned they were old enough to fend for themselves."

"Well, not quite," I corrected.

"So she showed up at the shelter this morning to surrender the kittens, but it was closed."

At this point, I was barely listening as I stared dully into the box of squirmy felines.

"But then she found your signature on the shelter paperwork and decided, and I quote, 'Since Dr. Reynolds can't tell a pregnant cat from a neutered male cat, *she* can deal with the consequences.'" Tiffany finally clamped her mouth shut with a satisfied grin.

I heaved a loud sigh. "You're kidding." I stared at her beaming face. "You're not kidding. I do hope you enlightened her to the fact that I did not examine that cat or sign that health certificate."

Tiffany shrugged. "I tried, but she had already dumped the box on the counter and bolted."

"Tiffany!" I groaned. "Why didn't you stop her?"

"The phone rang. I had to answer it because Rachel was on the other line."

I glared at her. "Well, I hope you at least got her name and phone number."

Tiffany did her best to look chagrined, but her effort fell short.

I thrust my hands on my hips. "Great! Now that woman thinks I'm incompetent! At worst, she'll sue me. At best, she'll slander my reputation to everyone at the grocery store, her church, and Pilates class."

"I'm sorry, Amanda. It all happened so fast. I was as shocked as you are." Finally, her expression softened into a more repentant one.

"Swell." I tried to think. Perhaps I could call Gary to see if he can locate the adoption paperwork. At least clear my good name. "What am I going to do with four—" I peered into the box and did mental calculations on their ages—"approximately three-week-old kittens?"

Suddenly, Tiffany remembered she had work to do. "Ooh, I've got to call a client back." She hopped up and tried to beat a hasty retreat out of the office.

"Whoa! Not so fast."

Tiffany froze, mid-step, her back still toward me, her shoulders sagging.

"Tiffany, you got me into this mess—"

She turned quickly. "I can't take them. I have three big dogs."

"So, you can keep them in the bathroom or laundry room or something."

"My landlord said no more animals."

"How's he going to know? It's not like you'll be walking them on leashes through the neighborhood."

"My roommate's allergic to cats."

I narrowed my eyes. "What roommate?"

She let out a nervous giggle. "Oh, didn't I tell you?"

"No, as a matter of fact, you did not. Since when do you have a roommate?"

Rachel poked her head into the office. "There's a call for you on line one from someone named Kip."

Tiffany vanished before I could blink.

With the way my luck was going today, Kip called to cancel our meeting. "Hello?"

"Did I catch you at a bad time?"

I realized that my less-than-enthusiastic greeting stemmed from my annoyance at Tiffany, not at him. "Oh. No. Sorry, I was distracted."

His brief pause created an uncomfortable silence. "Well, I won't keep you. I just wanted to let you know

I'm running a little behind. Could we push things back half an hour?"

"Yes, of course. I'll see you at seven." That would give me time to get home, feed Eleanor—who would absolutely disown me once she discovered four strange kittens in the house —and change into something more attractive than my scrubs, which didn't smell like dirty dog. I found my irritation fading as my mind ran through the possibilities in my wardrobe.

"You have a client in room two," Tiffany announced from the doorway, pretending like the box of kittens on my desk was invisible.

I rose and took the chart.

"So, who's Kip? Is he that hunky policeman? What did he say?"

My lips flattened. "Tiffany, would you be so kind as to set those kittens up in a cage with food, water, and a litter box? *Before* you do anything else."

She knew better than to argue, so without pressing for more details, she went to do as she was told. For once.

Chapter Fourteen

By six-thirty, I'd transformed from "overworked vet covered in fur" to "mildly presentable woman with hope." I'd gone home, fed Eleanor (who hissed, growled, and turned her back in silent feline judgment of the box of kittens I'd brought home), showered, and changed into my favorite jeans, a soft pink sweater, and the good earrings—the ones that didn't scream *trying too hard* but definitely whispered *maybe a date.*

I even dabbed on perfume. Eleanor sneezed twice and stalked off, which I took as a sign of approval. Either that, or I was on her permanent black list. I choose to believe in approval.

By seven sharp, I pulled into the parking lot of Perk Up Café, my nerves fluttering like butterflies who'd had too much espresso. I told myself it wasn't a date—it was just coffee. With a man. After work. Who had nice shoulders and made my stomach do interesting things.

Kip was already there, seated at a corner table, his jacket draped over the chair, sleeves rolled up. He looked unfairly good for someone who'd probably spent all day dealing with crime and paperwork. I waved, trying to look casual and not like I'd spent twenty minutes picking out earrings.

"Hey, Amanda," he said, standing to pull out a chair for me. Polite, old-school. Something I could get used to.

"Hi." My voice came out an octave higher than usual. I cleared my throat. "I, um, hope you weren't waiting long."

"Nope, just got here." He smiled that Robert Redford smile, the one that manages to be both disarming and adorable, and made my heart do backflips. "You want coffee? Or something fancier? They've got those frozen things with whipped cream and sprinkles."

"Coffee's fine." Though, given how fast my heart was pounding, maybe I should've asked for decaf.

He gave our orders to the barista and returned a few moments later with two take-out cups bearing the Perk Up Café logo and two chicken sandwiches. After I wrapped my hands around the warm cup, I gazed into Kip's blue eyes and felt a tiny, perfect moment of two people on opposite sides of a small table. Two people attracted to each other. Two people getting to know each other better. I let myself imagine how I'd describe this later if anyone asked about *our first real date.*

Then Kip ruined it.

"So," he said, taking a sip of his coffee and

leaning back. "I wanted to talk to you in person instead of on the phone. To catch you up on the investigation."

My imaginary violins screeched to a halt. "Oh. The investigation."

"Yeah." He took another sip, oblivious to the sound of my romantic bubble popping, and unwrapped his sandwich. "We've gone through the evidence from the shelter. Nothing new. Forensics didn't find anything helpful, and no witnesses have come forward."

I tried to smile, though my soul had just face planted. "So… no progress?"

"None worth mentioning." He looked at me, serious now.

Forcing a grin, I said, "So, do I need to rehearse my alibi?"

He chuckled, but it didn't reach his eyes. "That's actually what I wanted to talk to you about. To give you a heads up."

Oh. So not a date. My heart sank faster than a body weighted with cement shoes in a secluded lake. Poor metaphor, I realized too late. Or was that image a metaphor or . . . Geez, what difference did it make? *Focus, Amanda.*

I crossed my arms. "You're kidding, right?" The coffee I'd swallowed gurgled in my churning stomach. I pushed my still-wrapped sandwich away.

"Afraid not. The department is taking a closer look at everyone connected to Margot Dilly. Including you."

"But I barely even knew the woman."

His tone was apologetic, but steady. "You argued with her the day before she died."

"I've already explained all that."

Kip sighed. "Amanda, I'm not saying you did anything. But the chief wants to take another look. You had a disagreement with the victim, and you found the body."

I folded my hands on the table, trying to look composed while my inner panic mode short-circuited. "So, what exactly are you saying? Should I be lawyering up, or just practicing my prison slang?" I couldn't help the sarcasm that snuck into my tone.

"Look, Amanda, just keep telling the truth, and you'll be okay."

I threw up my hands. "I *did*, and look where it's got me."

"For the record, I don't think you did it."

"Gee, thanks," I muttered, then rethought my ungrateful response. At least, Kip was on my side. And I needed every police officer I could get on my side.

"And just a reminder. Please don't go poking around in the investigation. I know you talked to Jerome Finkle—"

"I've already explained that, too."

"—It'll only make things worse. For both of us."

There was something in the way he said *for both of us* that made my stomach flip. But before I could explore that interesting little development, he looked away, jaw tightening. The conversation was clearly over.

"So that's it?" I asked. "You asked me to meet you and got my hopes up that this was a date, just to tell me I'm a likely candidate for soon-to-be guest of the state?"

His mouth quirked at the corner. "You thought this was a date?"

My cheeks flamed at what I'd let slip, and I took a sip of my lukewarm coffee to avoid answering. Time for damage repair. I huffed. "As if I'd go on a date with someone who keeps threatening to arrest me."

He leaned in, eyes glinting. "Technically, I've never *threatened* to arrest you. But don't give me a reason."

Kip smiled—that slow, easy Redford smile again—and for a moment, I forgot that I was still under investigation.

Then his phone buzzed. He glanced at it, grimaced, and stood. "Duty calls. Try not to get into trouble, okay?"

Thoroughly humiliated, I simply nodded.

As I watched him leave, I muttered into my coffee, "So glad I wore earrings for this." I sat back and exhaled. So much for romance. Apparently, my love life and my criminal record were both under review.

When I finally made it home, Eleanor didn't greet me at the door. Great. She was still giving me the silent treatment. I found her guarding the bathroom door, tail twitching. I opened the door to a chorus of meows. Judging by the smell, they had found the litter box. Eleanor peeked from the doorway, her tail puffed like a bottlebrush, eyes blazing with betrayal.

"Don't even start," I told her. "I didn't *ask* for kittens. They were thrust upon me."

She hissed, stalked off, and jumped onto the kitchen counter for the sole purpose of knocking my mail onto the floor. Message received.

I addressed the mewling box of fur. "Well, at least one of us had some company tonight. I got downgraded from 'date' to 'debriefing.'"

One of the kittens—tiny, orange, and judgmental—looked up at me and squeaked.

"Yeah, that's what I said."

I gave them fresh water, cleaned up their mess, and then collapsed onto the couch with a glass of milk and my most comforting throw blanket. My mind replayed the evening with painful clarity—Kip's serious tone, his 'stay out of it' speech, and the part where he stood up to leave while I was still halfway through my coffee.

He could have *pretended* to be interested in my day. Maybe asked how many pregnant cats I'd misdiagnosed lately. At least start with small talk before jumping right in to "Me cop, you suspect."

Eleanor reappeared, hopped onto my lap, sniffed me disdainfully, and then turned her back.

"You're a real comfort," I muttered, scratching

behind her ears.

She yawned and jumped down.

By the time I got into bed, I had mentally rewritten my "coffee with Kip" recap at least five times—each version progressively more tragic.

In Version One, he swept me off my feet. In Version Five, he swept me off to jail.

Chapter Fifteen

Saturday morning was my turn to work, and since I'd been gone for a month, I couldn't very well call Dr. Barkley and ask him to cover simply because my body protested. Between Kip's warning last night and my general sense that the universe was out to get me, curling into a fetal position and putting my hands over my ears seemed like the best option.

Unfortunately, sick pets wait for no mental breakdowns. A brisk morning of skin infections, catfight wounds, and one particularly vengeful parrot who remembered me from his last visit kept me too busy to wallow. Even Tiffany's pointed "So, how was your date?" interrogation failed to break me. I sidestepped her questions with the skill of a cat avoiding a bath.

I'd just managed to take a break and grab a greatly needed cup of coffee when Vanessa called.

"Good morning," she said brightly.

"Why do I feel you're about to ruin my day?"

"I've set up a meeting for us this afternoon with Mrs. Meece."

I put down my coffee. "Vanessa, no. We are *not* meeting Mrs. Meece. Kip told me again to stay out of the investigation." I went on to tell her about his heads-up last night that the police wanted to talk to me again. Which sounded less like conversation and more like a pre-arrest warmup.

"Well, then we have no choice but to continue investigating," she replied. "Before they pin everything on you. Tighten the noose, so to speak."

"Vanessa, I can't—"

"Fine, think of our visit to Mrs. Meece as a social call."

"Social? You think she wants to drink tea with us and discuss plans for the yacht club ball?"

Vanessa ignored my remark. "She said she wanted to set things straight. That sounds promising, right?"

I groaned. "Vanessa, that sounds like *exactly* what Kip told me to avoid."

"Oh, come on. You said yourself the police are just spinning their wheels and circling back to you. What harm could it do to listen?"

"Listening leads to talking. Talking leads to questions. Questions lead to Kip showing up at my door threatening to arrest me for interfering."

I could almost hear her grin. "You like him."

"I didn't say that."

"You didn't *not* say it."

I rubbed my temples. "I'm not discussing my love life—or lack thereof—with you."

"Fine," she said breezily. "Then we'll discuss murder instead. Pick you up at three-thirty."

"Vanessa—"

But she had already hung up.

I glared at the disconnected phone. "If I get arrested for obstruction, I'm telling Kip this was *your* idea!"

At 3:30 sharp, Vanessa's Prius pulled up in front of my house. She leaned on the horn like we were fleeing the scene of a crime. Probably a poor simile, given the circumstances.

"I'm coming!" I yelled, rushing to grab my purse. I paused at the door to glance at the kittens, all lined up at the edge of their crate, staring at me like a fuzzy jury.

"Don't look at me like that. I'm not *investigating,* I'm just… attending a meeting."

Eleanor, perched on top of the fridge, flicked her tail like she didn't believe me either. *Sure, tell it to the judge.*

When I got into the car, Vanessa gave me a once-over. "You look awful. Did you get any sleep last night? What else has been going on that I don't know about?"

I told her about the kittens and how not only couldn't I sleep because of what Kip had told me the night before, but the kittens' meowing and scampering had contributed to my sleepless night as well.

"Cheer up. I may know of someone who will take a kitten."

"Really?" That news did perk me up. "How about four?"

She smiled. "Let me think on it."

Mrs. Meece lived in one of those gated communities where the entrance sign looked more expensive than my car. The guard waved us through after Vanessa flashed her dazzling smile and announced we were "from the animal shelter." Which was technically true, if not currently relevant.

The Meece mansion gleamed in the sun like it had been imported from Versailles—with manicured lawns, pastel stucco, and decorative fountains that screamed, *My husband has a wizard for a financial advisor.*

Vanessa parked, smoothed her hair, and whispered, "Okay, remember—friendly, non-accusatory, and if she offers anything to drink, say yes. Rich people notice that kind of thing."

The door opened before we even knocked. Mrs. Meece stood framed in the entryway, elegant in a cream silk blouse, gold jewelry, and enough perfume to qualify as a public health hazard. Her smile appeared genuine.

"Dr. Reynolds, Ms. Shaw. How nice of you to come." Her voice oozed sugar and control. "Do come in. I've made tea."

Tea. Of course. Because nothing says "potential murder suspect" like bone china and hospitality.

The house looked as if it had been decorated by someone with unlimited funds and whose Pinterest board was titled "Old Money, No Personality." Everything gleamed—glass, gold, and marble in quantities that made me afraid to breathe on anything.

Mrs. Meece gestured toward an ornate sitting room, where a tea tray and an assortment of gourmet cookies awaited. "Please, have a seat."

Vanessa sank onto the sofa like she belonged there. I perched on the edge like a housecat unsure of its welcome, praying not to spill anything worth more than my monthly mortgage.

Thank you for seeing us," Vanessa said smoothly. "We just wanted to touch base about the unfortunate issues at the shelter."

Mrs. Meece's smile didn't waver, though her eyes sharpened, as she expertly poured the tea and passed over the cups. "Yes. Issues. With that dreadful Margot. The woman had the manners of a feral cat."

I accepted my cup and saucer with a shaky hand. The porcelain felt so fragile, I was sure it could sense my Walmart mug energy. Any moment now, it would shatter out of rebellion for being forced into the hands of riff-raff.

Mrs. Meece laughed, but the mirth felt forced. "Can you believe she called me a bimbo?"

"Well," I said, "that was uncalled for and

unprofessional." I set the teacup on the pristine glass-and-chrome coffee table before dropping it.

Marilee narrowed her eyes and spoke to something over my shoulder. "Oh, I know what people say about me. They love to underestimate me. My husband is a wealthy man, and I'm twenty years younger, so obviously I must be a brainless gold digger. A trophy wife."

Well, yeah, there was that story. Especially when he divorced the first Mrs. Meece to marry the current one. I was fairly sure that "brainless gold digger" had been Marilee's unofficial title since the day she said "I do."

"But I'll have you know I have a master's degree in business administration," she announced, lifting her chin.

"Really?" Vanessa and I said in unison before we could stop ourselves. Whoa! Who would have thought?

"Yes, from Emory. That's how I met Ronald, you know." Marilee went on, as though this was common knowledge. "It was hardly a Cinderella story. I was heading up his Atlanta-based firm, and he came down for a meeting, and . . ."

A sly smile curled her lips. "Well," she said, drawing her attention back to us, "the rest, as they say, is history."

Yes, it was. The scandal, the messy divorce, the tabloids.

"We can't tell you how sorry we are for how

Margot treated you," Vanessa said. "Especially someone who has always been so kind and generous to unfortunate animals."

Marilee pursed her lips. "Her refusing to take in that adorable little dog that Harriet found really ticked me off. That was unconscionable."

We were saved from responding by a sudden thundering of paws that sounded like someone had literally "let the dogs out." Before I knew what was happening, a pack of undistinguished mutts burst through the French doors in utter mayhem. They descended on us, jumped on the designer furniture, clawed at the Persian rug, and made a beeline for the cookie tray. A pudgy, red-faced woman in a maid's uniform scurried in behind them.

"Oh, Madame! I'm so sorry. Someone left the kitchen door open and—"

"It's all right, Tina," Mrs. Meece said, laughing as one of the scoundrels jumped onto her lap and started licking her face, causing her perfectly coiffed hair to come loose in straggly tendrils. "Oh, my sweet babies! Mommy loves you, too."

I sat aghast as Mrs. Meece transformed from elegant hostess to unrecognizable, hair-tangled dog mom, and the mangy, undisciplined beasts ran amok through the showcase room.

Vanessa tried to fend off a massive pit-bull mix using a throw pillow like a gladiator's shield. She shot me a look that said both, "Would it be rude to push it off me?" and "Help!"

After what seemed like an eternity, Mrs. Meece rose and clapped her hands. All the exuberant canines stopped in mid-chaos and cocked their heads.

"Come now, we have visitors, and you are being very naughty." She led them out of the room like the Pied Piper.

Vanessa and I sat in stunned silence until she returned. Resuming her seat and attempting to pat her hair back into something resembling order, she said, "Sorry about that. They get so excited when we have guests over."

Excited? I worked with dogs all day. There was excited, and then there was *excited*. I was surprised they hadn't eaten the sofa.

Vanessa attempted to brush drool off her shirt. Somehow, I had a hard time envisioning the upper-crust elite guests of the Meeces being subjected to what had just occurred.

"Now, where were we? Oh yes. That dreadful Margot. She accused me of using my husband's money to 'buy influence' at the shelter. As if I needed to *buy* anything. I've been donating since before she even knew what a fundraising gala was."

I picked up my teacup, which miraculously had survived the invasion, and took a polite sip of tea— delicate, floral, and far too fancy for my tongue.

Vanessa regained her composure and smiled sweetly. "That must've been very hurtful."

Mrs. Meece's lips twitched. "I shouldn't say this, but I'm not sorry she's dead. As far as I'm concerned, she got what she deserved."

My eyebrows shot up. "Excuse me?"

Marilee gave a dismissive wave, the diamonds on her wrist catching the light. "Oh, come now. The woman was insufferable. I was going to stop supporting the shelter as long as Margot was in charge. Why throw pearls before swine? But then, the poor animals would suffer. So, I'm glad I don't have to make that choice. Problem solved."

"Right," I said carefully. "Well, we certainly understand your frustration."

She leaned back, studying me. "But don't worry. Now that she's gone, I will resume my contributions."

"That's very generous of you, Mrs. Meece." Vanessa reached for a cookie, then seemed to think better of it after the dogs had slobbered on them. Sitting forward, she asked, "Mrs. Meece, if you don't mind my asking . . . Would you have any idea of who might have wanted to kill Margot?"

If the question shocked her, Marilee didn't let on. "I would imagine just about anyone who had ever met her."

The impassive tone in her voice chilled me. How could a woman who loved animals so much be so indifferent to the horrific murder of a human? Even one like Margot.

"Why do you ask?" Her piercing gaze landed on

Vanessa.

"Oh, no reason," Vanessa said slowly. "It's just that . . . Oh, well, never mind. We shouldn't even be talking about this. It's an active police investigation, after all."

"Well, from the way I see it, whoever killed her did the world a favor." Mrs. Meece stood abruptly. "Now, if you'll excuse me, I have a yoga class to get ready for. And murder talk is bad for my chakra alignment."

Vanessa thanked her profusely. I managed not to trip over the Persian rug on our way to the door.

Once outside, I exhaled hard. "Did you see how weird she became when we started talking about the murder? It was as if she were completely devoid of all emotion. She changed from gracious socialite to ice queen."

Vanessa opened her car door and slid into the driver's seat. "She did act strangely. Like someone flipped a switch. I think we should tell Kip."

"Vanessa, we promised Kip we'd stay out of this."

"Technically, *you* promised Kip. I was never consulted."

I rubbed my temples. "Please, Van. I can't go to jail for interfering in a police investigation. I have four orphaned kittens at home."

"Fine. But in Marilee Meece's dog-eat-dog world, I'd rather be a dog."

Chapter Sixteen

As the ornate gates opened to let us out into the real world, my phone buzzed. The display read KIP GALLAGHER in all caps, as if he were already shouting at me.

I took a deep breath, whispered a quick prayer for composure (and invisibility), and answered. "Hey, Kip! What's up?"

"Where are you?" His voice was low and clipped. Uh-oh. Kip's "law enforcement" tone.

I shot a panicked look at Vanessa and tried to think of an answer that wasn't technically a lie. "I'm on my way home."

A pause. "You just left *Lakeview Estates*, didn't you?"

Blast. He'd probably driven by just as we were leaving Mrs. Meece's fancy gate. Small town. Big gossip. And Kip apparently had the ability to be everywhere at once. Kind of like Santa Claus.

"How did you know?"

Kip sighed — the deep, slow exhale of a man calculating how many times one woman could give him a headache before it became a medical emergency. "Amanda, we talked about this. I specifically said—"

"—that we should stay out of the investigation. Which we did! We just went by Mrs. Meece's house to apologize for the way she was treated at the shelter." I deliberately avoided any reference to Margot. "She's one of the shelter's biggest donors, and we need her support."

"And she's also a suspect in a murder investigation, in case you forgot."

"Well, there's that, too," I admitted. "But we weren't there to question her about the murder." I shot a warning look at Vanessa, who feigned pure innocence.

"Amanda, I was just on my way to question the woman again. When what do I see pulling out of the estate but Vanessa's car, with you riding shotgun."

"I can save you a trip. Mrs. Meece is on her way to yoga."

I could picture him pinching the bridge of his nose, probably resisting the urge to bang his head on the nearest wall. Or in his case, the driver's window.

"Look," I said, softening my tone. "We didn't do anything crazy. We apologized, admired her dogs, and left. And drank high-brow tea. She was friendly. Not psychotic."

Vanessa glared at me, and I shook my head. I

didn't want him to know we'd discussed the murder, as if he didn't already know.

"Amanda, I'm not going to tell you again—"

"I know. I know. But the reputation of the shelter is at stake."

"That's the least of your concerns right now. And for the record, I thought you didn't work there anymore."

"Well, I told Margot I quit. She's not there anymore, so maybe I'll un-quit."

His voice rose. "You may not have to worry about a job at all if you don't stop meddling in this investigation. I don't think anyone is going to bring their pet to the county jail for you to examine. Got it?"

I swallowed hard. "Got it."

"Good." He hung up without so much as a "have a good day."

I stared at the phone and then at Vanessa.

"He's mad, isn't he?" she asked.

"You could say that. I *told* you this was a bad idea. And really, what did we accomplish?"

"We learned that Marilee Meece has an MBA and is not an airhead."

I slumped in my seat. "Great, that will help a lot at my grand jury hearing."

The choir loft was meant to set the tone for worship, but this morning it felt more like the nerve center of a tabloid newsroom. I clutched my hymnal like it was a moral compass, though it was clearly pointing in the wrong direction.

"Did you hear about that awful murder at the animal shelter?" whispered Yolanda, leaning over from the soprano section behind me. "Oh, you must have, since you work there. Do you know any details?"

I turned toward her, raising one eyebrow. "We really shouldn't be discussing this in church. The service is about to start."

"Well," she said with a sniff, "I'm obviously concerned for all our safety. A murderer is running around loose in our town."

"I heard the woman was strangled with a leash from the shelter," said Kay, a bit too loudly.

Faith, our choir director, tapped her baton against the music stand. "Ladies," she said in a low voice. "Let's focus on *Blessed Assurance,* not *Dateline.* Sopranos, remember the rest in measure forty-three, please."

But focus was in short supply. Everyone wanted to talk about the murder—preferably in hushed tones that could still be overheard.

Chuck leaned in from the tenor section. "Is it just me," she murmured, "or do these sopranos seem way too cheerful about a homicide?"

"Misery brings community," I whispered back.

"You can tell me more after the service," he said, and I rolled my eyes.

Faith gave me the glare of a woman who'd endured twenty years of having to deal with singers like Stella Ramsey. "Amanda, if you have something to share with the group, perhaps you'd like to lead the anthem solo?"

I immediately found my page in the music and clamped my mouth shut.

After the service, I tried to make a quiet exit, but small-town churches have the same problem as *The Hotel California*—you can check out, but you can't leave.

"Well, Amanda!" boomed Pastor Dave, intercepting me by the coffee urn as I attempted to sneak out the kitchen door. "Terrible business, that poor woman at the shelter. You doing all right?"

"Just fine," I said, though my voice pitched up a notch. I cleared my throat. "Trying to keep my mind on higher things." I forced what I hoped was a convincing, pious smile.

Sister Bev, an elderly matron who materialized like gossip on legs, touched my arm. "We were just saying it's always the quiet ones. The ones you least expect. Who do *you* think did it?"

"I think," I said, scanning for an escape route, "that the Lord knows the truth, and He will guide the police to find it." I hoped. I shuddered to think of the gossip mill explosion if I were arrested. I'd be assigned a permanent seat in the choir next to Stella Ramsey as penance. Assuming I wasn't singing with the Dalton County Women's Prison choir.

Vanessa appeared at my elbow, mercifully steering me toward the door. "Come on, choir girl. Time to rescue your soul before someone starts a prayer chain with your name on it."

As we stepped into the bright morning sun, I sighed. "You'd think church would be the one place safe from gossip."

Vanessa snorted. "Sweetheart, if church people ever stopped gossiping, half the prayer requests would dry up."

We walked across the cracked asphalt toward my car, dodging potholes and parishioners. Mrs. Dempsey from the altar guild gave me a strange look. I smiled and waved, which probably just confirmed her suspicions that I knew something I wasn't telling.

"I hate being the center of attention." I unlocked my door and reached for my seatbelt as Vanessa climbed in beside me. "I could swear that Pastor Dave's wife was whispering about me during the anthem. She kept looking in my direction, and I don't think it was because of my efforts to drown out Stella." I started the car and eased out of the lot, narrowly missing a deacon who stepped into my path without looking. "But at least I haven't made the prayer list. Yet."

"Give it time," Vanessa said, smirking. "Someone's bound to lift you up before the week's out."

"Perfect. Maybe if the police hear about the persecution I'm enduring in the name of prayer for my welfare, they'll cut me a break."

"Doubtful. But take heart. I'll bring donuts to your arraignment. Chocolate glazed or sprinkles?"

"Both. I'm not counting carbs if I'm facing jail time."

We drove in silence for a moment, the laughter fading into the low hum of the air conditioner.

Finally, Vanessa said, "So, are we on for the council meeting?"

Chapter Seventeen

I'd just finished bandaging a schnauzer's paw the next morning when Detective Malone and his partner, Detective Rourke—the two detectives who had questioned me the night of the murder—darkened my clinic doorway. You could always tell the difference between clients and cops — clients came in clutching carriers and hope; cops came in with notebooks and bad news.

"Dr. Reynolds," Malone said, his smile polite but thin. "We need a few minutes of your time."

I sighed. "Does this count as a house call? Because my rates are higher for those." I smiled.

Neither laughed. That was never a good sign.

I motioned toward the break room and attempted another bit of humor to lighten the mood. "Can I get you gentlemen some coffee? It's strong enough to qualify as a controlled substance."

Again, not even a chuckle. These guys obviously had no sense of humor when it came to murder investigations.

They declined my offer, and we stepped into the office, where the crate of orphaned kittens batted at Malone's shoelaces. He looked down, and the stony expression on his face cracked just a hair. Kittens have that effect on a lot of people.

"Do you want a kitten, Officer? We're having a special today. Two for the price of one." I almost blurted out the story of how I came to acquire the brood, then thought better of it. According to the police, I already had enough grievances against Margot to commit murder.

Detective Rourke — mid-thirties, hair slicked within an inch of its life — opened a folder. "You were aware Margot Dilly was illegally selling animals from the shelter, including the parrot in the lobby?"

"Yes. But I found that out afterward. Which, I might add, is a terrible time to learn someone's been auctioning off your shelter mascot."

"Did you confront her?" Rourke asked.

I folded my arms. "Hard to confront a corpse, Detective."

His eyes narrowed. "Before she died."

"Oh. No. I didn't know anything about those dirty deals until after."

Malone flipped a page. "We've been going through the shelter's accounts. Some deposits don't line up. You handle finances?"

I let out a short laugh. "I can barely balance my own checkbook, let alone creative accounting. That was Margot's specialty. You should talk to Gary. He's found three different sets of books."

"And you know that how?" asked Malone.

Rourke jotted something down, which I didn't like one bit.

Oops. I tried to cover by going on the offensive. "Look, Detective, I worked with Gary for three years. I consider him my friend. Isn't it only natural that I talk to him about everything that's happened?"

"No. Not during an active investigation when everyone is a potential suspect."

"I want to circle back to the reason you were at the shelter on the night Ms. Dilly died," said Rourke.

I folded my arms across my chest. "I've already told you. I went to confront her about forging my name on medical records."

"You realize, Dr. Reynolds, that your stopping by the shelter to accuse her of something so damaging to your professional reputation on the night she died looks suspicious."

"Yes," I said evenly. "That's what happens when you're the one who finds the body. But if I killed her, would I have hung around and called the police?" Technically, I believe Kip was actually the person who called, but I wasn't going to complicate the issue with facts. Also, technically, it would have been hard to flee the scene of the crime with Kip flashing his badge at me. Still, I wanted to reinforce in their minds that I had done what any innocent citizen would do who came upon a murder. "Or would you rather I'd stepped over her dead body and gone home to watch Netflix, leaving someone else to discover the body?"

Malone shot me a warning look, the kind that said *sarcasm is not your friend right now.*

"Look," I said, trying for a calmer tone. "Margot was doing things with the shelter I didn't agree with. But I didn't kill her."

"You said you found Margot's body around eight-thirty that night."

"Right."

"And you didn't touch anything?"

Other than the mug of pens I'd thrown at Kip. "No."

Malone's expression didn't change. "You notice anything missing? Anything out of place?"

"Other than the leash wrapped around her neck?" I asked, unable to keep the cynicism from creeping into my voice.

They both remained silent, glaring at me with "cop eyes."

I sighed. "Sorry. Merlin was in a carrying crate on the table next to the desk."

"The bird she tried to sell."

"Yes."

Rourke closed his notebook. "We'll be in touch." He turned to go.

Malone lingered near the door, exchanging a look with Rourke.

"Actually, Doctor," he said, "there's one more thing."

There was *always* one more thing, as I knew from watching *Columbo.*

"We know you had words with Margot the day before she died."

I swallowed my frustration. "I've already gone over that. Several times. We had words, yes. Murderous intent, no."

"And you were angry."

"Of course, I was angry," I said, more sharply than I meant to. "But anger doesn't automatically make me homicidal."

"Depends on the person," said Rourke. "Margot seemed to have a knack for making enemies."

"Exactly!" I shot back. "As I've also told you, you should be talking to everyone else who was angry with her. The ones she stole from, cheated, and called nasty names."

Malone took a step closer. "We are. However, she had been making people mad for weeks. She was murdered the day after you returned to the shelter after having been gone for a month. The timing is quite the coincidence, wouldn't you say?"

That statement stopped me cold.

He went on. "You had motive and opportunity. You were there the night she died."

I drew a slow breath, forcing my pounding heart to calm. "And I've already explained that, too. Look, if you're looking for a confession, you're barking up the wrong tree."

The kittens in the crate mewed, their tiny voices cutting through the tension like a welcome reminder that not everyone in the room wanted me behind bars.

Emboldened by the injustice of being falsely accused, I said, "Why don't you question Merlin? He's an eyewitness."

Malone raised his eyebrows. "Merlin. The bird?"

My eyes burned into his. "Yeah. He can talk. Ask him."

"You've got a sharp tongue, Doc."

I stiffened my spine. "My sharp tongue is my weapon of choice. Not a leash."

The two exchanged glances once more, then turned to go.

"Don't leave town," Rourke said.

I rolled my eyes. "You do realize how cliché that sounds?"

"Cliches are cliques for a reason," he replied as they walked out.

"Let me know if you need a kitten," I called after them. Not that I would give either one of those men who wanted me in handcuffs a sweet kitten. I leaned against the desk, my whole body shaking from the encounter. Even the kittens had gone quiet, making the silence in the room feel like a heavy, strangling . . . YIKES! Not strangling! I had to clear my mind of that vision.

Tiffany appeared in the doorway, one eyebrow arched like she was daring me to confess to something.

"Well?" she said, tilting her head. "Did they believe you?"

I rubbed my temples. "Let's just say, if sarcasm were evidence, I'd be guilty as charged. They believe I had a motive."

She shrugged. "You did."

My head snapped up. "Excuse me?"

"Margot was ruining the shelter and your reputation. If I were you, I'd have wanted to wring her neck too."

I shook my head. "That's so not helpful, Tiffany. Please don't do me any favors by talking to the police on my behalf."

She donned a more sympathetic expression. "I'm sorry, Amanda. Really. Look, why don't you take a few minutes to pull yourself together? Dr. Barkley's almost done with surgery. I'll have him see the next patient."

I forced a thin smile. "Thanks." I slumped in my chair, listening to the soft hum of the clinic—the faint ticking of the wall clock, the hiss of the autoclave, phones ringing in the front office, and the kittens' small mews rising again, this time sounding more like comfort than chaos.

I bent over the crate and reached in, stroking their little heads. "Don't worry, babies," I murmured. "Nobody's going to arrest you. Just your innocent foster mom who was unlucky enough to be at the wrong place at the wrong time."

The kittens blinked at me, clearly unimpressed.

I settled back in my chair and stared at the ceiling. How had my life derailed so quickly? One week ago, my biggest problem was completing those ten spays and neuters at the shelter and worrying about whether I would continue working there with Margot as the new director. Now, two police detectives thought I was a murderer, my reputation was one rumor away from disaster, and my best defense was a parrot who couldn't testify.

Tiffany reappeared in the doorway. "Vanessa's on line one," she said with a snit, and I worried about her reconsidering telling the police I had a perfect motive for murder.

She lingered, arms crossed, as I picked up the receiver. I didn't have the energy to wave her off.

"I'm taking you to lunch," Vanessa said without so much as a hello. "We need to discuss our strategy for the council meeting tomorrow night."

"Uh," I muttered, glancing at Tiffany, who hadn't budged. "That sounds good. By the way, I'm inviting Tiffany to join us."

"You're what?" Vanessa's voice rose in a volume loud enough to carry across the room. Tiffany's jaw tightened.

"Yes, she's right here," I said sweetly. "And she says she'd love to come."

A sharp exhale of breath came from the other end. "Fine," Vanessa said. "We'll have to discuss our strategy later."

Chapter Eighteen

Tiffany and I slid into chairs at our table at the Marigold Café, and I tried to ignore Vanessa's withering look. The waitress took our orders and disappeared into the kitchen.

Frustrated by not being able to talk about her plans for the council meeting, Vanessa's attempt at small talk fell flat.

Tiffany, ever clueless, piped up. "The police questioned Amanda again this morning." A self-satisfied look settled on her face for being the conduit of news that Vanessa didn't yet know.

"What?" Worry lines formed in Vanessa's brow. "Why? What's going on?"

"Well—"

"Nothing. Just routine follow-up," I said, cutting Tiffany off.

The waitress returned with our food, and I hoped that would be the end of the conversation.

No such luck. "Routine?" Tiffany persisted. "But you said—"

"Oh, my goodness," Vanessa interrupted, staring over my shoulder. "Don't turn around too fast, but guess who just walked in. Myrtle Quackenbush."

Of course, I turned around. Myrtle was hard to miss in her silk scarf printed with koi fish, lipstick bleeding past the borders of her thin lips, and a permanent expression suggesting she'd smelled something unpleasant and couldn't quite identify the source.

I tried to avert my eyes and took a big bite of my hamburger, but it was too late. She zeroed in on me. "Don't I know you from somewhere?"

Should I play dumb? I chewed furiously while I debated.

"Probably from the animal shelter," Tiffany said helpfully.

I kicked her under the table. She made a wounded face at me that said, *What did I do wrong?*

"Oh, that's right. I saw you there the day . . ." Myrtle's voice trailed off, probably not wanting to acknowledge she'd been there to call out the suspected "other woman" and hoping I hadn't overheard her embarrassing exchange with Margot. She shook her head. "I heard about the unfortunate demise of that woman." Apparently, she couldn't bring herself to utter Margot's name. She sat, uninvited, in the empty seat next to Tiffany.

"Yes." Vanessa leaned forward, clearly in interrogative mode, pushing her plate to the side. "Things have been challenging for the shelter. The police are still investigating."

Myrtle waved a plump, manicured hand. "Stanley says it's a dreadful business, but he's confident the authorities will find the culprit soon. They always do, don't they?"

A beat of silence passed before Vanessa said, "Did you know Margot very well?"

"Not really. She was the shelter's director. Stanley helped her get the job."

"In light of how she mismanaged the shelter, I wonder why he would recommend her," said Vanessa, a look of pure innocence on her face.

Myrtle's mouth opened and closed a few times as she groped for a response. "Well, obviously Stanley was unaware of her . . . her incompetency and her—"

"Didn't you have a confrontation with her?" Vanessa persisted.

A blotchy red flush crept up Myrtle's neck. "No, just a minor misunderstanding, that's all."

"About what?" Vanessa asked, relentless as a terrier with a bone.

Myrtle huffed. "I don't believe that's any of your business."

"We heard your husband and Margot were having an affair," blurted Tiffany, and I choked on my iced tea. How did she hear *that* rumor? I'd been so careful.

The redness in Myrtle's face deepened to purple. "You are way out of line, young lady. As if my Stanley would risk his career and our marriage for that . . . that tart."

Unless referring to a dessert, I hadn't heard "tart" used that way for years.

"Sounds like you had some strong feelings against her," Vanessa said. She'd swatted at a hornet's nest. Not only did Myrtle not have a poker face, but she also didn't have a filter.

"She was a horrible person!" Mrytle shrieked, causing heads to turn. I slid lower in my seat. "Not only did she mismanage the shelter, but she also called my Stanley an old goat and called me a stupid old cow. What kind of civilized person says things like that?"

"That was quite unprofessional of her," I said quietly, hoping to calm Myrtle down and let people get back to their conversations. "And rude."

"I'll say. If I weren't a decent woman, I might have been tempted to throttle her myself."

Myrtle's statement hung in the air like a neon sign flashing *motive*.

Vanessa recovered first. "But of course, you'd never do something like that," she said lightly, dragging a French fry through ketchup.

The older woman sniffed. "Of course not. Stanley forbade me from setting foot near her again after the dreadful way she treated me." She seemed to be fighting to regain her composure after her public outburst. "Besides, she wasn't worth my time or energy. And I have a reputation to uphold as the chairwoman of the historical society. Good thing for me, I was at my bridge club on the night she was killed."

"Good thing," I echoed.

The silence stretched, broken only by the clatter of dishes and the buzz of conversation resuming at the other tables.

Finally, Myrtle stood, gathering her purse. "I seem to have lost my appetite. Honestly, I don't know how you girls can discuss such morbid topics during lunch. Good day." She swept out of the café, leaving behind a waft of Chanel and the distinct feeling she'd won a fight we didn't know we were in.

"Well." Vanessa popped another French fry into her mouth. "She certainly has no affection for Margot," she continued with her mouth full. "But she has an alibi for the night of the murder, so I guess we can rule her out as a suspect."

Tiffany stared at her. "Are you two investigating the murder?"

I brayed out a laugh as I stirred my iced tea, sloshing it over the rim of the glass. "Do we look like detectives to you?"

Tiffany's eyes ping-ponged back and forth between Vanessa and me. "I watch *Hallmark Movies and Mysteries*. The crime is always solved by someone other than the police. Can I help?"

"There's nothing to help with," Vanessa said too quickly.

"Who wants dessert?" I asked. "I'm buying."

A knock at the door jolted me upright. I hadn't realized I'd dozed off with my head in my hands during the afternoon lull. I half-expected to see Malone returning with handcuffs.

Instead, Kip filled the doorway, hands in his pockets, the familiar smile in place. "You look like you've been interrogated by the Spanish Inquisition."

"Close. The local inquisition. Rourke and Malone. With less charm."

He came inside and shut the door. Oscar jumped off my desk and weaved between Kip's legs, nearly tripping him. "So I heard. You shouldn't have been surprised. I told you they wanted to talk to you again. They're just doing their job, Amanda."

"Yeah? Funny how 'doing their job' feels a lot like building a case. Against me."

His expression softened. "You didn't make it easy. Sarcasm isn't the preferred dialect of innocence."

My chin shot up. "I was trying to stay calm."

The corners of his mouth twitched. "By provoking them?"

"It's a coping mechanism I use when I'm nervous. You should try it sometime."

Kip sighed and leaned against the desk. "Look, they've got to run down every angle. You had a motive, opportunity, and a connection to the victim. That's the bad news."

I huffed out a humorless laugh. "And the good news?"

"The good news is, I don't think they've got any real evidence tying you to the scene beyond being there."

"That's comforting," I said. "Maybe I'll embroider 'no real evidence' on a pillow, and they'll let me take it to jail with me." The sarcasm slipped out once more before I could stop it.

He smiled again, and my knees went weak. Good thing I was sitting down. "Just keep your head down for a few days. And if they come back, call me before you say something you'll regret."

"So, what, are you my lawyer now?"

"No, just a friend who doesn't want you to implicate yourself by opening your mouth and shooting yourself in the foot."

Did he just mix metaphors or something? Despite the direness of my situation, the image of blasting bullets from my oral cavity brought a flicker of amusement.

"That's a rather odd visual," I said, smiling.

"So? Sue me. I'm a cop, not a writer."

"And I'm a veterinarian, Kip. Not a mob boss."

"Could've fooled me." He winked, then turned to

leave.

I sat staring at the door through which he'd exited. Did he just flirt with me? Confusion ran in circles through my brain. What was up with him, anyway? Last week, he'd asked me to grab a burger with him, knowing I thought he was a felon out on parole. Then, he laughed in my face when I accidentally let slip that I thought our coffee meeting was a date. Was it okay for me to date criminals, but not him? Well, there was that sticky little matter that he was a cop investigating a murder in which I was a suspect, but what were these mixed signals he was sending? Was the man interested in me or not? And if not, he needed to keep his distance and stop flashing me that Robert Redford smile that made my legs turn to Jell-O. Still, his taking the time to come by without a warrant for my arrest and express concern for me showed some interest, right?

As the door clicked shut behind him, I exhaled and looked back at the kittens. One had managed to climb halfway up the side of the crate, mewing defiantly, as if daring gravity to stop it.

"Yeah, kid," I said softly. "Maybe you can teach me to navigate bars."

Chapter Nineteen

I hadn't planned to stop anywhere on my way home from the clinic. But after trying to function as a competent veterinarian while a murder rap hung over my head, my nerves were frayed like the new curtains Eleanor had shredded last week. I needed a distraction. Something to help me relax. Something, anything, to help me forget the suffocating tension that seemed to follow me everywhere I went. I parked in a shady spot and rolled down the windows so my crate of kittens could catch the faint evening breeze. Maybe with any luck, someone would steal the kittens from my car, and that would be one less thing I'd have to worry about.

The little boutique on Main Street—*Lavender Lane*—wasn't exactly my scene, but it sold locally made soaps, candles, and the kind of unnecessary luxuries that felt like emotional support purchases. I wandered in, inhaling the heady mix of lavender and vanilla, and let my hands roam over a display of delicate ceramic bowls and hand-poured candles. I had just lifted a lavender candle to my nose, savoring the faintly sweet scent, when the bell over the door jingled, and I heard the unmistakable lilt of Marilee Meece's voice.

"Oh, Dr. Reynolds, hello again."

Marilee glided over in a cloud of floral perfume, wearing enough jewelry to light up a small town. "Have you heard any more about the—" she looked around and lowered her voice—"situation at the animal shelter?"

"No," I said, not wanting to discuss the "situation" in public. The conversation with Myrtle Quackenbush at lunch had been quite public enough. Besides, Vanessa and I had already talked with Mrs. Meece, and I didn't imagine I would glean anything more from discussing it further. More importantly, I wasn't about to feed the town's ever-hungry gossip mill.

She leaned in, conspiratorially. "The rumors have been simply relentless. It was all anyone could talk about at Harriet's this afternoon."

"Harriet?" The name sounded familiar, but I couldn't place it.

"You remember. My hairdresser. The one who found that adorable little dog that Margot refused to take in." She wrinkled her nose.

"Oh, yes." Besides church, beauty parlors were the place to get the most up-to-date information in small towns. They were often better informed than the police. "Have you tried these?" I asked, waving the pale pink candle in front of her, hoping to divert Marilee from the subject of murder.

Her eyes lit up. "Oh, my, yes. Those are simply to die for." She gave a delicate laugh. "Speaking of dying, the police questioned me about the murder. Can you believe it?"

"They're questioning everyone who had any contact with Margot." I conveniently left out the part about my own lengthy interrogations. I also left out the part where I had mentioned Marilee's argument with the deceased to the police, probably pointing them in her direction.

She placed a manicured hand on a slim hip. "But honestly, do they know who I am?" This time, Marilee's laugh held a brittle edge as she flared her nostrils in indignation. "And the man who questioned me was that kennel boy, Kip! I mean, what's up with that?"

"Actually," I said, "Kip is a police officer. Surely, he showed you his badge. He was working undercover at the shelter."

"Well, that just goes to show that Margot was deeply involved in something criminal. People who get themselves mixed up in nefarious activities often come to a bad end." She waved her manicured hand dismissively. "Anyway, I'm sure it'll all blow over soon. The police have to look *somewhere,* don't they?"

I nodded, forcing a small smile while my stomach tightened. Somewhere. Somewhere that had my name on it.

Marilee's eyes flicked around the boutique, landing on a basket of hand-painted soaps. "And these, Dr. Reynolds," she said brightly, "are absolutely divine. I'm thinking of hosting a little soirée—invite the ladies from the shelter to take our minds off that dreadful business. I'll give these soaps to all the guests. Everyone will simply *love* them. You will come, won't you?"

Her invitation sounded more like a demand. "Sounds lovely," I said, my voice just steady enough to hide the tension threading through my limbs. "And please call me Amanda."

"Oh, excellent!" Marilee beamed. "It's always fun to support local businesses, isn't it?"

"Yes," I said. "Very fun."

She gave a final, tight smile, tilted her head as if assessing a piece of fine art, and then floated toward the cash register, a handful of soaps clutched in her fist. The scent of lavender that had felt comforting moments ago now seemed almost suffocating.

I set the candle down and pressed my hands to the counter, trying to steady the tight knot in my stomach. Marilee's words echoed in my mind: *"People who get themselves mixed up in nefarious activities often come to a bad end."* The way she had said it—light, airy, almost joking—made my stomach twist.

It wasn't the statement itself. She hadn't said anything directly. It was the *way* she said it, like she knew more than she should. Like she applied the words to me as well as Margot. Or perhaps my overwrought nerves were playing tricks on me. I needed to get out of this over-scented store and breathe some fresh air.

The shop assistant, a young woman with a cheerful bob and a name tag that read *Clare*, smiled at me. "Can I help you find anything?"

I shook my head. "No, thank you. Just… browsing." My voice sounded hollow even to me.

I wandered toward the door, trying to shake the tension out of my shoulders. I dug in my bag for my keys and my sunglasses, nearly tripping over a parking bump, and started walking toward my car. Just what had people discussed that afternoon at Harriet's?

Chapter Twenty

I went home without any overpriced emotional support purchases to help me relax. But then, what had I been thinking? I had the greatest natural serotonin dispensers known to man waiting for me in a crate in my car—four kittens. I defy anyone to hold in a smile while watching kitten antics. Well, except for Eleanor, who hissed and bolted to the bedroom when I opened the crate to let the kittens play.

Plopping onto the sofa, I purged my mind of everything but the joy of watching the tiny felines in action. Having been cooped up all day, their energy screamed for release. They tumbled across the living room like tiny, over-caffeinated acrobats, each one determined to outdo the others in sheer enthusiasm. I wadded a piece of paper into a ball—a cheap, convenient source of entertainment, and they launched themselves at the ball with all the grace of furry cannonballs, skidding halfway across the tile before popping back up as if nothing had happened. One tired of the game and clawed its way up the table leg just inside the door, where it discovered its reflection in the mirror overhead. It drew back in surprise, then puffed up and began shadow-boxing with great seriousness—punches wildly ineffective. Meanwhile, the others gave up on the paper ball and chased, pounced, and toppled over one another in an unending loop of delight. If serotonin had a marketing department, these four would be the poster children—pure, unfiltered joy wrapped in fur, paws, and unapologetic mischief.

Eleanor emerged from the bedroom and leapt onto the back of the couch, regarding the frolicking felines with pure disdain. Perched like a gargoyle, her tail flicked in slow judgmental sweeps, each one a silent commentary on the chaos below. Her emerald eyes narrowed to elegant slits as the kittens tumbled past in a blur of fluff and enthusiasm, and she drew herself up even straighter, as if good posture could protect her from their contagious foolishness.

"Oh, Eleanor," I said, laughing, as I gave her regal head a rub. "You don't have to maintain your dignity at all costs. Have you so quickly forgotten your humble beginnings?"

She answered with a low, aristocratic growl. Clearly, she disapproved of such silliness.

"If you don't lighten up, I'll get the laser light out. Then we'll see how fast you lose that haughty attitude."

My few moments of mindless bliss quickly dissolved when my phone chirped, and I saw Vanessa's number pop up. I tried to scoop kittens back into their crate—an act that felt like trying to collect dandelion fluff in a windstorm—and swiped the call button.

"This better be good. I was right in the middle of kitten therapy."

"You do realize that I'm one of the few people who actually understands what you're talking about, right?" Vanessa paused for a beat, then changed the subject back to where I didn't want to go. "We've got to discuss our strategy for confronting Stanley Quackenbush."

I closed my eyes. "You know, Van, the more I've thought about it, calling out an elected official at a public meeting isn't exactly subtle."

"Subtle?" Vanessa huffed. "Subtle left the building when we found out about his criminal activities with Margot. If we don't bring his corruption to light, he may very well appoint someone else besides Gary to take Margot's place and continue skimming funds designated for animal care."

I walked to the kitchen to prepare Eleanor and the kittens' dinner, then pulled a microwave meal for myself out of the freezer. "But we don't have any proof, other than what I overheard."

"That's enough to start with. Besides, I doubt his dirty dealings are limited to the shelter. He probably uses his position in a hundred other ways to funnel taxpayer dollars into his pocket."

Vanessa was most likely right. We owed it to the city to expose this bad apple's misdeeds. But my cowardly streak dug in its heels. We had already talked to several people, at the high cost of getting me out of my comfort zone—compared to which, Belize had been nothing by comparison—not to mention being threatened with obstructing an ongoing police investigation.

She went on. "We've also got the books Gary found."

"Well, actually, the police have those. What if we tip their hand before they have a chance to question him? It might give Quackenbush the time he needs to come up with a good lie."

"Look, you're a respected professional in the community. You *heard* him. And confronting him publicly may be the only way to force an investigation. At the very least, get people to see him through a different lens. Start planting those seeds of doubt so that even if the police can't pin anything on him, the public will think twice about re-electing him."

Eleanor had gobbled her dinner and rechecked the food bowl again. I hoped she didn't regurgitate from eating so quickly. The presence of the kittens had revealed a competitive side in her.

"Fine," I said. "But you still aren't thinking about wearing disguises, are you?"

"No, I'm thinking more along the lines of something authoritative. Professional, yet intimidating."

"I'll check my wardrobe for intimidating," I said. As if. About the only ones I could intimidate were Chihuahuas, and even then, they put up a good defense by going on the offensive first. I didn't bother to bring up what really worried me—the nagging suspicion that Stanley had killed Margot, and I was about to poke a nest of vipers with a big stick.

Chapter Twenty-One

I thought I managed to side-step Tiffany's curiosity fairly well the next day. Being overly busy with unscheduled emergencies helped. Of course, it was Dr. Barkley's day off because, naturally, chaos only respects *his* calendar. First came the Goldendoodle, who ate an entire table centerpiece—the ribbons, the flowers, the Styrofoam base, and, judging from the shimmer around his muzzle, possibly some glitter. When I palpated his distended abdomen, he let out a loud belch with a whiff of vanilla candle. Since there was no way for all this foreign material to pass on its own, I had to perform an emergency gastrotomy.

"Lovely," I muttered as I lifted the scalpel. "If I find a seasonal wreath in here, I'm charging extra."

The moment I pulled out the first wad of fake flora from his distended stomach, I wrinkled my nose. "Ugh. This doesn't smell anything like *my* florist's shop."

"I hope Mrs. Murphy has something else she can use as a centerpiece," said Tiffany as she bagged up the stomach contents. "I don't think she can resurrect these."

"She may not be able to afford a dinner party after she pays for this tummy tuck," I said, taking one more swipe around to ensure I'd gotten every craft-store ornament.

As I began closing the abdomen, Tiffany returned, arms crossed, weight shifted, the universal sign for *you're not going to like this.*

"You have another emergency waiting—Buffy Gossman. He's limping."

"That's hardly an emergency," I said as I placed my next suture.

"It is to Mrs. Gossman. She's afraid Buffy has cancer."

I snorted, which made my surgical mask billow. "Mrs. Gossman always thinks Buffy has cancer. Remember when she brought him in for the blotchy purple spot that turned out to be from her toddler coloring him with a magic marker? Or when he had yellow pine pollen on his belly and she thought it was liver cancer? Or when she came in hysterical about the 'asymmetrical' lump on his side that turned out to be matted fur?"

"She says she's been up all night with him."

Sighing, I said, "Tell her I'll be done in about ten minutes. If Buffy's waited all night, he can wait another ten minutes." As Tiffany left the room, I pondered why, if Mrs. Gossman had truly been up all night with her deathly ill Pomeranian, hadn't she brought him in first thing this morning? Then again, I was pretty certain her weekly pedicure appointment ranked somewhere just above "impending dog doom." To say the woman was a tad high-maintenance was an understatement. But, on the bright side, she always paid her bill.

I finished closing the incision, laid my instruments on the stand—after removing the scalpel blade—unclamped the surgical drape, and stepped back from the table. After calling Tiffany to recover the dog, I pulled off my gloves, gown, mask, and cap, and took a moment to stretch my aching back, which let out a creak that sounded like it was lodging a formal complaint. It was only ten o'clock, and I was already wishing the day would end. Unfortunately, the council meeting tonight loomed over me like a raincloud with a bad attitude.

Plastering on my most "concerned veterinarian" face, I stepped into the first exam room where Mrs. Gossman sat hugging Buffy like he was providing emotional support for her, rather than the other way around.

"Oh, Dr. Reynolds, thank *goodness* you're here. I just *know* Buffy has cancer this time. He's holding up his right front paw."

"And when did this start?" I asked, readying my clipboard to take notes.

"Last night. I tell you, I'm so upset I couldn't concentrate on anything this morning until I could get him in."

My eyes shot to her perfectly polished toenails peeking out from her sandals. Perhaps pedicure therapy helped her relax. I wouldn't know. I'd never had a pedicure in my life.

"Mrs. Gossman, as we've discussed many times, cancer rarely appears suddenly like this. It's more likely Buffy has a minor injury."

"But you *will* take an X-ray to be sure?" Two frown lines appeared between her meticulously plucked brows. "I've read about dogs breaking bones from bone cancer."

"If necessary. Let me look at him first."

She relinquished the little fluff ball, and he shot me a look that said, *Thank you for being normal. Please save me.* I picked up his front foot and immediately saw the problem.

"It's not cancer," I said with a smile. "Buffy has torn a toenail. We'll take care of that in a jiffy."

"Oh!" Her hand flew to her throat. "Oh, thank goodness! You have no idea how worried I was."

"Let me just borrow him for a minute and take him into surgery."

The word was out of my mouth before I realized my mistake.

"Surgery! But you said it wasn't serious."

"It's not." I rushed to reassure her. "I just need Tiffany to hold him for me, and she is currently watching another patient recovering from anesthesia."

I hustled out of the room before she could engage me in more theatrics.

Tiffany sat cross-legged on the surgery floor beside the groggy Goldendoodle bundled in warming blankets like a canine burrito. She glanced up.

"So, what's the catastrophic illness this time?"

"Torn toenail." I handed him to her while I reached for the nail clipper. She rolled her eyes.

Buffy didn't even whimper when I snipped off the broken nail tip and applied some styptic powder. In fact, he looked grateful. I placed a light bandage on the paw and returned him to his owner, who thanked me as though I'd performed open-heart surgery with knitting needles. I wished all emergencies were so straightforward.

I had barely grabbed the top chart for the four patients who had been waiting through the surgery when Rachel, our receptionist, strutted into the treatment area with the righteous indignation of someone whose coffee had been made incorrectly by Starbucks.

"Dr. Reynolds, you didn't charge Mrs. Gossman a during-hours emergency fee. You didn't even charge her an exam fee." She placed a hand on her hip as disapproval dripped from her expression.

"I know." I sighed. "I couldn't bring myself to charge those fees for a simple broken toenail." Squaring my shoulders, I said, "But I did charge for the nail repair and the bandage."

Her eyes narrowed. "This is why I never get a raise. You need to let Tiffany put in the charges."

"Tiffany was busy."

"Yeah, yeah," she muttered as she turned to go. "By the way, a lady is bringing in her bird. She says it has a hole in its head."

I stared at her. "How did her bird get a hole in its head?"

She shrugged. "Beats me. That's why you get paid the big bucks, and I don't."

I knew Rachel was only half-kidding. Staff members knew that most veterinarians were their own worst enemies when it came to charges.

After taking care of the first patient, I entered the findings into the computer. Tiffany suddenly materialized at my elbow, startling me so that I almost smacked my nose on the screen.

I shot her a look. "What?"

With three more patients waiting, surely, she could have made herself useful.

Tiffany squinted at me. "You're acting weird today."

"I— what? I'm not acting weird. I'm up to my eyeballs in emergencies and a waiting room full of patients, *as you can plainly see.*"

"I'm not talking about that. I'm talking about how you've got that guilty wrinkle between your eyebrows that you always get when something is going on. Or when you've eaten my yogurt."

I pressed the print button for the exam report. "I did not eat your yogurt. I'm just *busy*."

"Something is going on."

I sighed. Tiffany could sniff out secrets like a border collie tracking a contraband ham sandwich. "It's nothing. Could you please start the intake on the next patient?"

Tiffany stood planted to the floor. Suddenly, her eyes lit up. "I know what it is! It's the council meeting tonight, isn't it?"

I took a sip of my cold coffee and tried not to choke.

"It is! Seeing Mrytle Quackenbush yesterday reminded me."

I silently cursed myself.

"It's about Stanley Quackenbush. You think he's involved in the murder, and you're going to confront him, aren't you?"

I tried to deflect her. "Why would I do that? The police are investigating him. I'm a veterinarian, not a detective."

"Because they are also investigating *you*." She got that self-satisfied smirk that she always wore when she knew she was right. "Well, I'm going with you."

I froze. "Tiffany, that's really not necessary. We are only going to sit quietly. Listen. Observe. No scenes. No drama."

"We?" Her expression turned sour. "Oh, as in Vanessa and you. Without me."

Drat! My big mistake. My mind was too addled to lie effectively. Yes, theologically, I knew that God disapproved of lying. He had written it in stone, after all. But He would surely forgive me for a little misdirection when it came to Tiffany, wouldn't He?

"Tiffany, let me re-emphasize. We don't want any drama."

"Oh, and I suppose I create drama?"

I stared at her. *Keep mouth shut.* "Look, I just don't want things to escalate."

"Escalate?" Tiffany leaned in close. "Amanda. Everything involving Stanley Quackenbush is rife with corruption and drama."

I groaned. "Tiffany, please—"

"I'm coming," Tiffany declared. "End of discussion."

I could see I was fighting a losing battle. "Only if you promise to behave."

Tiffany nodded solemnly, hand over heart. "I promise I will behave."

"This is going to be a disaster," I muttered under my breath.

Tiffany beamed. "It's going to be *amazing*."

Rachel interrupted. "Your bird with the hole in the head is here. I put it in room two."

I shot Tiffany an annoyed look. Because of her persistence, I was now running further behind than ever. I left her standing there as I stomped off toward the second exam room.

"Good morning," I said, forcing cheer into my voice as I greeted the distraught owner. "I hear Crackers has a . . . hole in his head?" I bent to examine the beautiful blue-front Amazon parrot sitting peacefully in its cage. No blood anywhere. No sign of trauma. No obvious hole. Just one very chill bird. Straightening up, I faced the owner, Miss Willingham, a thin, fluttery woman who stood wringing her hands.

"I can't imagine what happened," she said. "I was just petting his head, and *there it was.*"

"Can you show me?"

She took a deep breath, opened the cage, and lifted Crackers out. Thankfully, he cooperated, saving me from the usual parrot rodeo of chasing him all over the room with a towel, uttering swear words in my head. With a careful finger, she parted the feathers on the side of his head.

"See? It's right there."

I tried to hold in my laughter, but failed. "Miss Willingham," I said gently, "that is his ear canal."

Her eyes widened. "His *ear*?"

"Yes. Birds don't have an external ear flap like other animals. Look," I said, brushing the feathers away from the other side of his head. "Matching set."

"Oh!" A bright red flush crept into her face. "I feel so foolish. I was *so* upset. How could I not know it was his ear?"

"It's okay, Miss Willingham. If it makes you feel any better, you're not the first bird owner who's discovered a cranial hole that turned out to be normal avian anatomy."

Her tense shoulders dropped two inches. "Well, that's a relief. Thank you so much, Dr. Reynolds."

"You're welcome. And there's no charge for today."

As I walked out, I could already imagine Rachel's reaction when the invoice popped up blank. Rachel would have a hissy fit.

Chapter Twenty-Two

I slid into my seat next to Vanessa at City Hall, my heart pounding like I'd run a marathon instead of just walking in from the parking lot with a lukewarm Diet Coke.

She pointedly looked at her watch. "It's about time. The meeting is getting ready to start."

I looked around at the roomful of people, relieved not to see Tiffany among the crowd. Maybe she was at home watching reruns of *The Hallmark Mystery Channel*, taking furious notes on how real detectives confront suspects, and got so engrossed in the plot that she forgot the time. Nevertheless, I plopped my purse on the empty seat next to me.

Vanessa's eyes narrowed. "Why are you saving a seat?"

I stalled, hoping Mayor Buford "Buck" Crenshaw would call the meeting to order and rescue me. No such luck. His head was bent in an intense conversation with Councilwoman Natalie Tatum, who looked like Marilyn Monroe had cloned herself and run for office.

Men adored her. Her IQ, however, would be ten points higher if she were a rock.

Clearing my throat, I said, "For Tiffany." I lifted a defensive hand before Vanessa could explode. "I couldn't help it. She knew about the meeting and insisted on coming."

Vanessa huffed out a frustrated breath. "It's not that I dislike Tiffany, but she's the antithesis of subtle. It will be hard to catch Quackenbush off-guard when she's like the marching band you can hear from three blocks away trying to sneak up on you."

"Well, it's not like either of *us* has a plan," I muttered, twisting around to scan the room again. "We're strictly shooting from the hip. Anyway, I don't see her. Maybe we—"

"I have a question for Commissioner Quackenbush," came a familiar voice from the back of the room.

I groaned.

Heads turned. The council members looked up.

"Miss, the meeting hasn't started yet," snapped Mayor Crenshaw, visibly annoyed at having his discussion with Natalie disrupted. Then, glancing at his watch, he sighed. "However, we're a few minutes late in starting, so I suppose we'd better get going."

He banged his gavel against the table with gusto. "I now call this council meeting to order. Before we address new issues, Councilman Harmon will give us an update on the sewer issue."

As a lanky, elderly councilman rose and began his lengthy, monotone dissertation on the bowels of the city, Tiffany slid into place beside me, a huge grin on her face.

I leaned over and whispered into her ear, "We're here to observe. Quietly. No drama. You promised."

A look of frustration crossed her features. "But how are we going to—"

A woman in front of us turned and glared at us.

I placed my index finger against my lips. Tiffany crossed her arms and slumped in her chair. As I tuned out the sewer report, movement flickered in my peripheral vision, and I groaned for the second time in five minutes. Kip. Our eyes locked for a moment, and a distinct warning showed in his. I opened my eyes widely in innocence. With any luck, maybe someone else in the audience would address the question of the murder, and we three stooges could sit quietly and unobtrusively.

Councilman Harmon finally wrapped up his sewer saga. "Any questions?"

Tiffany's hand shot up. "I have a question."

The councilman peered over the top of his bifocals. "Yes. The young lady in the second row. Would you stand up and identify yourself, please?"

She hopped to her feet. "My name is Tiffany Purcel, and I would like to ask Commissioner Quackenbush about the murder at the animal shelter."

Councilman Harmon looked momentarily

perplexed as his head swiveled to his fellow councilman. Stanley's face flushed, but he shook his head and shrugged his shoulders.

Harmon turned back to Tiffany. "Miss, we are currently addressing the sewer—"

"I'd like to know more about the murder, too," said Vanessa, shooting to her feet on my other side.

"Yeah," said someone behind me. "We're all concerned about the murder. Forget the pipes."

"Did you know, Commissioner Quackenbush, about the illegal activities that were going on at the shelter?" Vanessa demanded.

So much for subtle. And Vanessa accused *Tiffany* of being dramatic. I sank lower in my chair, praying for a cloak of invisibility.

"What illegal activities?" a man called from the back of the room.

The mayor banged his gavel, but it had about as much authority as a wooden spoon at a frat party.

Vanessa turned around to address the man's question. "Margot Dilly was stealing people's purebred dogs and selling them."

A collective gasp went through the audience.

"And," Vanessa went on, "she was skimming money from fund-raising events."

Now, everyone began to talk at once, the meeting quickly becoming out of control.

"Why did you hire Ms. Dilly, Commissioner Quackenbush?" Tiffany asked, raising her voice to be heard among the cacophony.

"Order!" thundered Mayor Crenshaw, repeatedly banging his gavel.

Commissioner Harmon looked utterly lost. Finally, he sat back down, obviously disappointed that his sewer report was receiving little attention.

Questions ricocheted around the room.

"Commissioner Quackenbush? The young lady asked you a question," said a middle-aged woman to the right of us. "Why *did* you hire Ms. Dilly?"

Stanley's mouth opened and closed several times as all eyes turned to him. His flush deepened to crimson, and he tugged at his necktie as though it strangled him like the leash around Margot Dilly's neck.

"Is it true you were having an affair with her?" shouted Tiffany.

Before Stanley could deny the charge, Mrytle Quackenbush jumped up like her pants were on fire. "Absolutely not! How dare you impugn my husband's reputation?"

"Then, is it true you were in on the money skimming with her?" yelled Vanessa.

Mayor Crenshaw banged his gavel once more, and—crack— the head flew off, narrowly missing a gentleman seated in the front row.

Stanley's panicked eyes darted to his right and his left, begging his fellow commissioners to stop the pandemonium that had broken out.

"Of course not!" bellowed Stanley's wife. "How dare you accuse—"

"We have proof to the contrary," insisted Vanessa, further fanning the flames.

"What proof?" Someone's voice carried across the uproar.

"A set of books Margot Dilly kept." The din swept away Vanessa's words, much to my relief.

For the love of all things municipal, don't mention the books! It's our only ace in the hole. I tried to telepathically convey my thoughts to Vanessa, since there was no way she would ever hear me whisper them.

"Did you kill Margot Dilly?" Tiffany hollered.

Commissioner Quackenbush finally lurched to his feet, a momentous accomplishment considering his girth, and the noise gradually died down. Everyone sat in eager expectation of the man's response to the allegations. He swallowed, and I saw his Adam's apple bob in his thick throat.

"I resent these slanderous accusations," he said stiffly. "My reputation speaks for itself. I have nothing more to say." He pushed back his chair and strode out the side door.

The crowd surged after him, leaving the rest of the stunned commissioners, the mayor, the three of us, and, most notably, Kip, in the room.

Vanessa and Tiffany seemed to have bonded over their ambush of the commissioner, as they high-fived each other over my tense shoulders.

"I think we got him," said Vanessa, a smug look on her face.

Tiffany laughed. "We sure got the people talking."

I glared at both of them, which required extra coordination since they were flanking me. "What happened to subtle? Not tipping our hand?"

"Amanda, you have to admit that people are going to want to know how deep his involvement is in all of this," said Vanessa. "Even if he didn't kill Margot, the voting public needs to know he's a crook."

"Yeah," echoed Tiffany.

I didn't have time to react to their crowing because Kip was already heading our way—slow, deliberate, his body language radiating, *You're in trouble.* His expression said he was a man whose patience had run out somewhere around the middle of the sewer report. We could've made a run for it, but his eyes delivered a crystal-clear command. *Sit. Stay.*

The smiles slid from my companions' faces as they registered his approach.

"Ladies," he said quietly, which sounded more intimidating than if he'd yelled. "A word."

It wasn't a request.

Kip herded the three of us into one of the small conference rooms off the lobby, the way a weary ranch hand might wrangle three rogue goats. The second the door clicked shut, he planted his hands on his hips and stared at us—*stared*—like he was trying to decide whether to scold, lecture, or just bang his head into the wall until retirement.

No one spoke. *Now* my two friends decided to go mute. Where was this resolve ten minutes ago?

Finally, he exhaled a long, suffering groan. "What," he said slowly, "in the name of common sense was that?"

Vanessa crossed her arms. "We were gathering information." Her chin jutted up.

"You were inciting a riot," Kip shot back. "A literal riot. I had people climbing over the backs of chairs trying to chase an elected official."

"Well, technically, they were just seeking answers," Tiffany offered helpfully.

Kip closed his eyes like he needed a moment to pray for patience—or possibly a transfer to a different county. Or country.

"You three turned a straightforward council meeting into an episode of *Cops: Municipal Edition.*"

I lifted a hand timidly. "In our defense, we meant to be subtle."

That did it. Kip barked out a laugh—one sharp, humorless burst. "Subtle? Amanda, subtle would've been sitting quietly and listening. Subtle would *not* have included shouting questions about affairs, embezzlement, or murder before the Pledge of Allegiance."

Tiffany opened her mouth to protest, but Kip

pointed at her. "No. Don't even. You accused a commissioner of murder during the questions and answers of the sewer report."

"Well, we all *wanted* to know," she said, gesturing wildly. "The public—"

"Oh, don't hide behind 'the public.'" Kip rubbed his forehead. "The public also wants free donuts and shorter lines at the DMV. That doesn't mean they get them."

Vanessa huffed. "We got people talking."

"Yes. About lynching a councilman." He scrubbed a hand across his face. "You three have to let us handle the investigation. *Us.* The trained professionals."

"We were just trying to help," Vanessa grumbled.

"And you're doing it loudly," Kip said. "And publicly. And wrongly. And in a way that makes me age in dog years."

He looked at me then—really looked—and I could see exhaustion under the frustration.

"Amanda… you have to keep them in line."

I spread my hands, palms up, in a position of surrender. "I think that's above my pay grade."

"It absolutely is," Kip said. "But apparently nobody else can do it."

There was a long silence.

Then Kip straightened, running a hand through his hair, as if bracing himself for whatever fresh chaos awaited him outside the door.

"Listen carefully," he said. "From here on out, no more stunts. No more ambushes. No more interrogations, hints, nudges, insinuations, suggestions, or interpretive dances insinuating guilt." He looked between Vanessa and Tiffany. "You two stay out of the spotlight. And out of trouble."

Tiffany nodded vigorously. "Of course."

Vanessa nodded too. "Absolutely."

Kip stared at them for a beat. "That's the most convincing lie I've heard all day."

He opened the door, paused, and added over his shoulder, "Now I've got to go answer for this mess to the mayor and the council." The door swung shut behind him.

Tiffany looked at us. "So… does that mean we're grounded?"

Vanessa shrugged. "He didn't say we couldn't *observe*."

I groaned. "Please stop talking."

But I knew—even before Tiffany's eyes lit up— that they absolutely would not give up.

I just leaned back in my chair, rubbing my temples. "Next time, I'm hiding in the supply closet."

We reconvened in the parking lot in Tiffany's SUV, exhausted but buzzing with adrenaline. Tiffany tapped her fingers on the dashboard like a metronome, counting down until the next disaster.

"Okay," she said, eyes bright, "so the meeting *totally* went off-script, but people are talking. That's good, right?"

I groaned and flopped into the passenger seat. "Sure, if your goal was to terrify the mayor, humiliate the council, and make Kip rethink every career choice since kindergarten."

Vanessa stroked her chin. "We need a plan. A real one. One that doesn't involve yelling murder accusations in public or risking getting banned from City Hall."

Tiffany tilted her head, which worried me, since it appeared she was thinking. "We just go to plan B. You know…the one Kip doesn't know about."

I groaned again. "Plan B? Do I even *want* to know?"

"Of course you do!" Tiffany said, twisting around to face me. "It's brilliant. Elegant. Totally subtle."

I narrowed my eyes. "You just said the word 'subtle.' You know that's not your style."

"Exactly! That's why it'll work. Nobody will see it coming!" Tiffany grinned.

I stared at her. "You're making no sense."

"Trust me," she said. "We need to keep the heat on Quackenbush, but we can't get Kip furious again— or he'll literally chain us to the kennel runs."

Kip's glare when he assigned me to take charge of these two fixated and delusional women flashed through my brain. I would never forget that look.

Tiffany leaned back, hands behind her head. "Okay, team. Step one: gather intel without causing a public incident. Step two: keep the pressure on Quackenbush and hope he cracks. Step three: profit—or at least survive."

"Surviving is good," I said. "You *do* recall a murder actually took place. This isn't a game, Tiffany. I think we should stay out of this mess and let the police do their jobs."

"Until they arrest you," muttered Vanessa. "Then where will you be?"

Suddenly, the idea of a quiet cell where neither Vanessa nor Tiffany could whisper unwise courses of action into my ear sounded appealing.

Chapter Twenty-Three

The next morning dawned way too early, as I debated on dragging my weary body out of bed. I already dreaded the day ahead. I don't know what we accomplished last night, aside from inciting a potential riot. Or, for that matter, I didn't know what we'd achieved with any of our meddling short of incurring the wrath of a man I would really like to impress. I let loose with an unladylike snort. I'd impressed him, all right. Kip was probably ready to haul me off in handcuffs just to keep me out of the way.

The kittens, not caring about the drama that had become my life these last few days, meowed loudly for their breakfast.

"I'm coming," I grumbled, forcing my resisting body from the comfort of my nice warm bed.

When they saw me, they became even louder. "I've got to find homes for you guys while you're still little and cute."

I opened a can of cat food, which sparked Eleanor's interest, as I pretty much fed her dry food. "Fine, you get some, too." I dished hers out first, then set the kittens' bowl in the crate, where the kittens climbed over each other to beat their siblings to the bounty. "Slow down, there's enough for everyone."

Despite the heaviness of the past few days, I couldn't help but laugh at their antics. Kittens are a natural mood elevator and cheaper than therapy.

My phone buzzed as I headed to the shower. Who would be calling so early? Glancing at the screen, I saw Vanessa's number pop up, and I braced myself. She wasn't exactly a sunrise and roses kind of person.

"Hey, Van," I answered. "Please tell me you're calling at this hour to tell me they have Stanley Quackenbush in custody and he's singing like a canary. Or quacking like a duck."

"Sorry. No waterfowl confessions that I know of yet. I was calling to see how you were after last night."

I sighed. "I'm okay, but I'm done with all the subterfuge. I just want my old boring life back."

"Good, because I have just the thing to take your mind off everything for one day."

Despite my initial wariness, my curiosity piqued. "What did you have in mind?"

"My nephew's pee-wee soccer game tonight. It'll be fun watching those little kids play. You can even invite Tiffany if you want."

Now my radar spiked. "Tiffany? Are you serious? You don't get along with Tiffany, remember?"

"Actually, I think we worked pretty well together last night, since you were determined to sit like a bump on a log."

"I was trying to—"

"Besides, we both care about you."

I gave in. "Okay. How about if Tiffany and I meet you at the soccer field after work?"

"Six o'clock. The game has to be over by seven so the kids can get into bed."

"See you then." But she'd already hung up. Why did the uncomfortable feeling that Vanessa was up to something cling to me like static-charged cat hair to black leggings?

Tiffany, of course, was delighted with the invite, so happy she didn't even prattle on about the disaster we'd caused at last night's council meeting. I found myself honestly welcoming the distraction. At that point, I'd have taken any mind-numbing entertainment short of spelunking in a sewer with Councilman Harmon if it meant thinking about something other than murder and suspects.

By the time we arrived at the soccer field just before six, I spotted a familiar figure standing on the field holding a tiny soccer ball in one hand and a clipboard in the other, grinning for a dozen cameras as a gaggle of kids ran in circles around him. Stanley Quackenbush.

I was going to *kill* Vanessa! Might as well charge me with double homicide. How many life sentences could I get?

Tiffany clutched my arm. "Okay…we need a plan. Quick, quiet…something *subtle-ish*."

Vanessa approached with an expression so innocent it could have been packaged as organic and gluten-free.

I thrust my hands on my hips. "Cut the act, Van. You knew perfectly well Quackenbush would be here."

Her eyes grew round. "No, I didn't. I swear."

"Are you willing to testify to that in the prayer group on Sunday morning?"

She hesitated. "Well, now that I think of it, I *may* have heard my nephew mention that Stanley sponsored their team."

"Van—"

"But it slipped my mind. I swear."

"Again, I ask, are you willing to testify to that—"

"Okay! Fine! But we didn't get any satisfactory answers from the man last night, and here, he can't escape."

Before I could argue, Quackenbush's sharp eyes landed on us from across the field. His smile vanished. The clipboard in his hand pivoted like a weapon.

"Well, well, well," he said, voice carrying easily over the field. "If it isn't the city's very own amateur detectives. Out here to harass me now?"

Tiffany grinned like a puppy who had just learned a new trick. "We're just…fans! Big fans! Of your…uh…soccer skills."

I rolled my eyes. Vanessa muttered, "We might want to reconsider calling ourselves fans."

Quackenbush's lips pressed into a thin line. "I am the team *sponsor,* not the coach. Your antics are…truly over the top."

Tiffany dropped the grin. "We just want answers!"

He stepped closer, his voice low enough that only we could hear. "You want answers? Then, schedule an appointment like any normal person would. Not whatever ambush this is."

And you'll be eternally unavailable per your poor secretary's instructions.

Vanessa's spine stiffened. "For your information, Commissioner, my nephew plays for this team. We didn't know you'd be here. Everything isn't always about you, you egotistical—"

"I suggest you three leave, before you give me a reason to file a lawsuit *today*, in front of witnesses, at a public event." His small eyes narrowed, disappearing into flabby folds.

"*Leave?*" Vanessa shrieked. "It would break my nephew's heart if I didn't watch him play in the opening game."

As if on cue, a blue-jerseyed moppet with "Stanley's Stallions" printed across the front barreled toward us and wrapped himself around Vanessa's waist. I guess "Quackenbush's Quahogs" was too long to print on a small jersey.

"Aunt Vanessa, I *knew* you'd come!" He beamed up into her face.

She ruffled his already chaotic dark hair, a springy mass of curls just like hers. "Of course, Liam. And I brought my friends. You remember Amanda, right?"

He stared at me for a moment before a smile lit up his face. "Yeah, you're the vegetarian."

I chuckled. "Close, Liam. It's pronounced 'veterinarian.' But you can just say 'animal doctor.'"

"And this is Tiffany," Vanessa said, turning to her new BFF.

He held up a shy hand. "Hi. Thanks for coming. Gotta go." Then he zipped back to his teammates' huddle.

Vanessa turned back to Quackenbush and thrust out her chin. "See? This is a public park, and you can't make us leave. We're staying for the game."

"Yeah," Tiffany echoed. "Why are you so paranoid, anyway? Unless you have something to hide."

A cloud descended over his already stormy face. He jabbed a pudgy finger at us. "Just stay away from me, or I'll file a lawsuit for harassment. And maybe a restraining order." Then he turned and stomped toward the team bench, his politician smile nowhere in sight.

I shot a look at Vanessa. "Well, that certainly answered a lot of questions."

She shrugged. "It was worth a try."

I threw up my hands. "He's a *politician,* Van. He's not going to say anything incriminating."

"Let's hit the snack bar and watch the game," said Tiffany brightly.

I did my best to enjoy the game. But it was hard to concentrate on five-year-olds kicking each other in the shins when every thirty seconds Commissioner Quackenbush whipped around to glare at us like we were plotting his downfall.

Which, technically… we were.

Or—a chill ran down my spine—he was plotting ours.

Chapter Twenty-Four

I suppose it should have come as no surprise the next morning when Kip showed up carrying an official-looking envelope as if it were radioactive.

Inside was a letter from a lawyer— Marlon Everson Wainwright, because why have one pretentious name when you can have three—announcing that Stanley Quackenbush was suing me for harassment. Tiffany had an identical one, complete with threatening legal jargon and enough pomp to choke a Rottweiler.

We retreated to the office, where Kip planted his hands on his hips and shook his head. "You just had to do it. You just couldn't stay away from trouble, could you?"

Heat crawled up my neck. "Now just a minute, Kip. We went to watch Vanessa's nephew play soccer. We never said a word to Quackenbush. *He* approached us and told us to leave."

"And you had no idea that he'd be there?" he

asked, squinting at me like I was a toddler caught with a fistful of cookies. "As in you weren't stalking him?"

"No!" Tiffany and I said in unison. At least *we* hadn't been. Vanessa's version of events might have required creative editing, but thankfully, she wasn't present to incriminate anyone, particularly me.

"That's the truth," I said. I blew out a frustrated breath. "So, what are we supposed to do? Call ahead to every public place in the entire town to make sure Stanley Quackenbush isn't lurking? This is ridiculous, and you know it!"

His stern cop expression softened into something a little less intimidating. "For what it's worth, I don't think he'll get anywhere with this lawsuit. The only one likely to make out from this show of muscle is Marlon Everson Wainwright."

"So, what should we do?" I asked. "Do we need to hire a lawyer? We can't afford that."

"You don't know any lawyers?"

"Only Buddy Brown who Battles Like a Bulldog. He's a client."

Kip rolled his eyes. "I don't think an ambulance chaser is your best bet, unless Quackenbush injures you somehow."

"Well, then who?" Tears stung my eyes. Last night wasn't even our fault. Vanessa had set Tiffany and me up.

"You can always represent yourself."

"Against a smooth-talking politician and his

shady lawyer?"

"How do you know Marlon Everson Wainwright is shady?"

"With a name like that, plus his association with Stanley, he has to be."

Kip sighed. "Let me ask around."

Relief flooded over me, and I had to restrain myself from throwing my arms around his neck. "Thanks, Kip."

But Tiffany was far from ready to drop the subject. "So, where is this investigation going with Stanley? Have you examined the shelter's books yet?"

Kip frowned. "You know I can't discuss an ongoing *police* investigation with you. Notice I used the word 'police.'"

"But have you questioned him? What has he said?"

Kip arched a brow. "As I just said, I can't—"

Tiffany slammed her letter onto the desk, making a sad, papery thwip, but still conveying her displeasure.

"So, are we just going to rot in jail while that . . .that criminal walks the streets bilking taxpayers and maybe killing people?"

A smile tugged on the corners of Kip's mouth. "Tiffany, you don't go to jail for a civil offense. Didn't you read the letter? He's asking for $25,000 in damages. From each of you."

Her lower lip began to quiver. "I don't have $25,000. Even if I sold everything I own."

"Don't worry too much. Quackenbush is just blowing smoke to make you back off. Which, by the way, I told you to do several days ago."

Before he could warm up to that lecture, I gently steered him toward the door.

"Thanks again," I said, trying not to drown in his gorgeous blue eyes. How I wished those eyes weren't always looking at me with equal parts frustration and disappointment.

He patted my shoulder. "I'll be in touch."

The moment Kip left, Tiffany and I stood in stunned silence, still clutching our legal-threat letters as if they might bite. We barely had time to exchange a look before Dr. Barkley appeared in the doorway, arms folded, brow furrowed, and wearing the familiar expression of a man who has just realized his carefully planned clinic schedule is circling the drain.

"Ladies," he said in that measured, deceptively calm tone he reserved for fractious cats and staff emergencies. "Do either of you plan on working today, or should I just start telling clients the staff is temporarily tied up in litigation?"

Tiffany sniffed and waved her letter like a flag of surrender. "Stanley Quackenbush is suing us! For twenty-five thousand dollars! *Each!*"

Dr. Barkley stepped fully into the office, closed the door behind him, and let out a sigh long enough to qualify as medically significant. "I heard. Kip filled me in on his way out." His gaze softened. "I'm sorry you two got dragged into this mess."

I sagged into a chair. "We didn't do anything wrong. We were just watching a soccer game."

"I know," he said gently. "But knowing you didn't do anything wrong doesn't magically clear the waiting room."

He tapped the stack of charts he was holding against his palm. "Since eight o'clock, I've had two dentals, one blocked cat, and Mrs. Dempsey calling to ask why no one has called *her* yet. You know how she gets."

Tiffany groaned. "Please don't mention her right now. I can't handle Mrs. Dempsey and a lawsuit in the same day."

"I'm not blaming you," Dr. Barkley said quickly, hands raised as though defusing a bomb. "I'm just saying the chaos level has officially exceeded my daily allowance. I care about you both—but I also care about not drowning in paperwork and irate poodle owners."

I rubbed my forehead. "I'm sorry. I don't know how this situation snowballed so far out of control."

"I understand," he said. "At first, I found your involvement somewhat humorous, even if it was ludicrous. But now it is starting to interfere with the clinic's operations, what with the police coming and going. I am asking that for the rest of today, you try— just *try*—to avoid any additional scandals, crimes, civil suits, or municipal uprisings. At least until after lunch."

"We didn't start this," Tiffany mumbled.

"No one is accusing you of starting anything," Dr. Barkley said. "But trouble seems to have your home address lately."

I opened my mouth to argue, but he held up a finger. "Don't. Please. I'm on my last nerve. And I need both of you. The clinic needs both of you. So if you're going to battle Quackenbush, do it on your lunch break."

He softened then, his tone shifting from exasperated boss to concerned mentor. "Look, if you need assistance paying for legal counsel, I can help with that." He laid a hand on our shoulder. "We'll get through this. I know you're worried. But Kip's right—you don't need to panic. Nevertheless, for the love of veterinary medicine… no more field trips."

He turned toward the door, paused, and added, "Also, the Goldendoodle who ate the decorative candle centerpiece vomited up something purple. So, whenever you're ready to work again, congratulations, that's your case."

Tiffany's shoulders slumped. "I hate purple."

"Get your gloves," I said. "Purple waits for no one."

Chapter Twenty-Five

We managed to make it through the rest of the workday without any more drama—at least related to the murder. Just the usual veterinary drama, like the parrot who'd come in for a simple nail trim wiggling loose from Tiffany's arms, doing three flight laps around the room, and then wedging itself inside the ultrasound machine. *Inside.* I never knew I had the skills to disassemble and reassemble the machine. At least I hope I reassembled it with the correct number of screws it started with in the proper places. My ten-minute appointment turned into forty-five.

Then came the Persian cat who managed to fall face-first onto a sheet of sticky fly paper. To say she was not happy with her veterinary care would be an understatement. She screamed like she was being flayed alive before I even touched her. I'm sure the waiting room clients were googling "urgent care animal clinics open now."

And the Goldendoodle? He'd acquired yet another festive centerpiece—this one featuring realistic-looking purple berries. Hence, the purple vomit decorating the exam room floor. Two radiographs later, I confirmed that his stomach was, blessedly, empty-ish and that most of the berries had been deposited on our linoleum, leaving a purple stain. I diplomatically suggested the owner reconsider her commitment to home décor. Thankfully, that crisis resolved itself before I had to re-operate. But at least I would have had a dotted line from the previous surgery to follow.

By the end of the day, I had almost managed to relegate the pesky lawsuit to a dusty back shelf in my brain.

"I'm done in," I announced to Tiffany, as we attempted to scrub the resistant purple stain from the floor. "Don't even think about asking me to go out and get into trouble. I'm going to go home, lock the door, eat junk food for dinner, take a nice long bath, get in comfy pajamas, and watch the dumbest TV shows I can find." Which shouldn't be hard.

"Me, too," she said, quite uncharacteristically.

"I might even turn off my phone."

Her eyes widened. "Gracious, you *are* serious."

"You bet I am. I said I was done with all this amateur detective business, and I meant it. If the police want to pin Margot's murder on me, so be it. At least, I'll get a nice long rest in jail, three meals a day that I don't have to cook, and no client calls."

She gave me a sad smile. "I'm sure this will all blow over soon. Even this stupid lawsuit." Giving me a wave, she disappeared out the back door.

I was two steps away from freedom when Rachel intercepted me like a linebacker. "There's a Mrs. Meece on the phone for you. She says it's urgent."

Now what? I couldn't take much more today. I picked up the extension.

"Mrs. Meece? This is Dr. Reynolds. What can I do for you?"

"Oh, thank goodness I caught you before you left. I have another little stray dog who needs to be admitted to the shelter, but Gary's already left. Can you possibly meet me there and take her in?"

I held in my long-suffering sigh. "I'm sorry, but I don't work there anymore."

"Ohhh." She stretched the words into three pitiful syllables. "Oh, dear. I don't know what I'll do with this dog. I don't have anywhere to keep her in the house, and I'm afraid that if I put her in the yard, she'll escape. She's so tiny."

"Let me try to reach Gary," I said. "I have his cell number."

"Oh, that would be wonderful. Thank you so much."

"Give me your number, and I'll call you right back."

I quickly entered her information into my phone, then pressed Gary's number. "Please pick up, please pick up."

His voicemail answered with a cheery, "Hi! You've reached Gary. I'm unable to take your call at this time, but—"

Drat. I punched the end-call button with more force than was necessary. Why couldn't Mrs. Meece simply put the dog in one of her twenty bathrooms for the night? Maybe I could call her back and make that suggestion.

"Hello, Mrs. Meece," I said when she answered on the first ring. "I'm afraid I couldn't reach Gary. Why don't you put the dog in a bathroom or laundry room for tonight, where she won't escape, and drop her off in the morning?"

"Oh, I'm afraid if I do that, she'll bark all night, and my other dogs will go crazy knowing she's in the house. My husband and I would never get any sleep."

It was no use. The woman was rather eccentric and wealthy. A combination that ensured one got her own way.

"All right. I really shouldn't do this, but I still have a key. I will meet you in the back parking lot in ten minutes."

"Oh, thank you, Dr. Reynolds. That is so kind of you."

I held in my annoyance. After all, a few minutes out of my way wouldn't make much difference. I could do a quick exam, admit the dog, and leave a note for Gary. I didn't think he'd mind.

Stepping into the kennel, I corralled my four feline charges into their crate. On a positive note, three people had expressed interest in adopting them just today. After this weekend, I could probably let them go.

"Come on, guys, we've got one quick stop to make, then we're heading home." I exited the clinic, locking the back door behind me, and placed the crate in my car. I would have to take them into the shelter with me, as the day had turned brutally hot—too hot to leave them in the car. Great. Breaking and entering with witnesses.

Mrs. Meece and I pulled up at the same time—her in her gleaming BMW, me in my eight-year-old Corolla. She emerged wearing an expensive-looking white sundress now patterned with smudges from the stray dog she clutched like a newborn heir to the Meece fortune. I walked around to the passenger side of my car and unloaded the crate.

"I can't tell you how much I appreciate . . . Oh? What do you have in there?" She stooped to look through the bars. "Oh! Kittens! How adorable. Where did they come from?"

"It's a long story," I muttered, not wanting to get into the details.

"Do you have homes for them yet?"

"Yes, for three of them," I said. "Actually, three people expressed interest today."

"Oh! I want the last one."

I blinked. "You do?"

"Yes. Please save it for me. I don't care which one."

My mood lifted. This trip had proved productive after all. Eleanor would be so glad. I bit my tongue to keep from asking how all of Marilee's dogs would handle a kitten. Not my problem.

We walked to the back door, and I inserted my key, taking a furtive look over my shoulder to be sure nobody spotted us. Technically, I wasn't supposed to be here. It would be just my luck that someone like Stanley Quackenbush would be driving by and report me to the police. I opened the door and ushered Mrs. Meece inside after flipping on the lights.

"Let's go into the office and let me get the paperwork," I said.

She smiled and trailed me to the office, where I tried, once again, not to shudder. Forcing the disturbing murder scene from my brain, I reminded myself that I had been in the office with Vanessa and Gary since the murder, and no ghosts had jumped out at me.

"Have a seat while I look for the intake forms."

Marilee sat daintily on the chair across from the desk, one long leg crossed over the other, jostling the little dog on her lap as though it were a baby. She sat taking in the surroundings as though she'd never seen them before.

"I'm so glad Gary is taking over as director. He's such a nice young man."

I popped my head up from rummaging through

drawers. Of course, Gary had rearranged things to suit himself. "Yes, although for now, he's only the temporary acting director."

"Well, I certainly hope the commissioners don't allow Stanely Quackenbush to hire someone else. He sure made a mess of things by hiring that . . . that horrible woman."

I kind of had my doubts that the commissioners would allow *that* mistake to happen again. "I'm sorry it's taking so long. I can't seem to find . . . oh, here they are."

Pulling out the folder, I sat back in the leather chair, noting that Gary had replaced the one where Margot had met her untimely demise. I took out a form and handed it across to her along with a pen and a clipboard.

"If you'd fill out the information you have—"

"Yes, yes, I know the procedure." She waved a dismissive, beautifully manicured hand and began filling out the form. "I don't really know what breed this little darling is."

"That's okay. We'll make our best guess after we get her cleaned up."

"Can you believe she was found hanging around the dumpster at Joe's Chicken Shack?" Mrs. Meece made a clucking sound with her tongue. I wasn't sure whether it was out of sympathy for the dog or because of the mention of chicken. "Poor little thing. I bet somebody dumped her."

"May I ask how you got her?" I certainly didn't envision Marilee Meece dining anywhere near Joe's Chicken Shack.

"Oh, a young lady who works there brought her to me this evening. She knew I had a connection with the shelter."

Of course. Money always had connections. She finished the form, and I flipped the paper over to go through a quick medical evaluation.

"If you wouldn't mind holding her for a minute, let me run get a stethoscope and otoscope from the surgery suite, and I'll do a quick physical."

"Certainly." She kissed the top of the dirty head, leaving a smudge of red lipstick behind.

I walked out of the office and down the hall. As I turned on the lights in the lobby, Merlin perked up. "Hello, beautiful."

Pausing briefly to scratch his head, I murmured, "Hello, Merlin. I've missed you."

He leaned into his massage and said sweetly, "I love you."

"Well, I'm glad somebody does. And I'm glad to hear you've cleaned up your vocabulary. At least I hope you have. I'll come back and spend a few minutes with you before I go, but right now, I've got to take care of some business first. Okay?"

I should have felt silly explaining myself to a birdbrain, but as a person who talks to animals for a living, I didn't. At least Merlin could talk back.

After fetching the needed equipment, I returned to the office with the encouragement from Merlin in the form of a wolf whistle.

"Here we are. Just hold her like that while I look her over."

I did a brief exam, found nothing amiss, and laid my instruments on the desk. "Okay, then, let's get her settled into a run for tonight, and I'll let Gary know about her first thing in the morning."

Marilee hopped up, carrying her precious cargo and murmuring to the dog in reassuring baby talk.

As we walked back through the lobby on the way to the kennel, Merlin exploded in a loud screech.

Marilee jumped, almost hurtling the dog across the room. "Good gracious! What in the world?"

"Merlin," I said, stepping over to the cage. "It's all right, baby. It's just us."

His pupils dilated, and his feathers puffed defensively. Then he slammed his wings against the cage. "Help me! Help!" he shrieked.

"Merlin, what's wrong?" I opened the cage and reached in to see if I could calm him down. I didn't want him to hurt himself.

"Stupid bimbo!" he screeched. "Stupid bimbo! Help me!"

My hand froze. The sarcastic words I'd thrown at Malone and Rourke about questioning Merlin, their only eyewitness, came back to me in jarring clarity. Merlin *had* been an eyewitness to Margot's murder.

And for some reason, he was *very* agitated by the presence of Mrs. Meece.

I turned and studied her face, which had gone ashen.

"Let's get this dog settled," she said, her voice trembling over Merlin's raucous screaming. "I . . . really need to be getting home."

For a long moment, I just stared at her, not sure whether I wanted to be alone in the kennel with her or not. Or, for that matter, the deserted shelter, with our cars parked out back where nobody would see them. I groaned inwardly at my thoroughness in keeping this meeting clandestine.

"Please, can you make that bird be quiet?" She sank into a lobby chair and put her head in her hands. The little dog slipped from her lap and took refuge under her chair.

I rolled Merlin's cage into the surgery suite off the lobby. Part of me, the sensible part, said to barricade myself in the room and call the police. Then I remembered there was no phone in the surgery, and my purse with my cell phone was in the office.

Quickly, I looked around to see what I could use as a weapon. I could fill a syringe with a sedative and try to poke her with it, but the keys to the controlled drug cabinet were in my purse in the office. Besides, I'd have to get close enough to her to inject anything, and then pray she didn't kill me before the several minutes passed for the sedation to kick in. Maybe I could douse a surgical cloth with an inhalant anesthetic and press it against her nose and mouth. But again, I'd have to get close to her and be able to overpower her, which, given her apparent strength at taking down Margot, I wasn't sure I could accomplish. Plus, with my luck, I'd breathe in more of the anesthetic than she would and end up passed out on the floor, where she could easily finish me off.

Scalpel? No. Hand-to-hand combat again. Besides, I didn't think I had it in me to ram a scalpel into another person, not even in an emergency. But I couldn't stay holed up in surgery all night. There was no exit to the building from this room, and she could easily corner me in here. The only thing I had to fight with was my wits. Hah! That was a comforting thought. With any luck, maybe Marilee had escaped and was halfway across the state border by now.

Against my better judgment, I stepped back into the lobby. No such luck. She sat in the same place with a vacant look on her face. She now knew I knew the truth. But perhaps I could still play dumb.

"Marilee, were you here the night Margot was killed? Did you see something?" Maybe that would give the woman a clear out, and we could both walk out of the building as though nothing had happened. All she had to do was say she'd been here and Merlin had seen her in the office, but Margot was alive when she left. Who was going to take the word of a bird over hers? Then I could pretend I believed her, flee to my car, drive away, and call Kip.

"I didn't mean to kill her," she said, her whispered words distorted by her hands, and I wasn't sure if I had heard them correctly. Ice water shot through my veins, and my heart slammed against my ribs. Scratch that plan.

She lifted her face, tears streaking her makeup. I didn't run. Couldn't. My feet had grown roots and planted themselves to the floor. Besides, the exit was behind her.

"I just came here that night to try to reason with the woman. I didn't want to sever my relationship with the shelter. You know how much I love the animals. But she was *so* unreasonable. And so awful. She never cared about the poor animals she was supposed to be helping." Marilee's voice cracked, and she went on. "She laughed in my face and called me a stupid bimbo again. Do you know how those words affect me?"

So, you killed her because she called you a name? *Move, Amanda! Don't just stand here!* But I still couldn't move. I found myself doing something I should have done long before getting myself entangled in this mess. Prayed. *Oh, God, I wouldn't blame you if you left me to suffer the consequences of all my ill-advised decisions over the past few days, but if You could find it in Your heart . . .*

Marilee swallowed hard. "I've lived with the stigma of being called a dumb blonde all my life. Something just snapped, and I grabbed the nearest thing

I could find—a leash lying on the desk. The next thing I knew, I had it wrapped around her neck, but before I could pull it tight, she started screaming for help. I knew I couldn't back down at that point. She would tell the police I tried to kill her and . . . " Her voice trailed off.

Every hair on my body stood up.

For a few seconds, all I heard was Merlin screeching from the next room and the frantic thrumming of my own pulse in my ears. Marilee sat frozen, arms wrapped around herself, eyes wide and shimmering.

"I didn't pull hard," she whispered. "Not at first."

"Marilee," I said as gently as my terror would allow, "you didn't plan to hurt her. This is something the police—"

"No!" She stood suddenly, taking a quick step toward me.

I stepped back. A completely rational, instinctive, backward shuffle. My ankle bumped a mop bucket that had been left out to dry, and the clatter echoed like cannon fire.

"Please," she said, voice cracking. "I didn't *mean* to kill her. I didn't. But the next thing I knew, she was just . . . just slumped in her chair. I didn't know what to do. I panicked and ran out the door."

"Okay," I said, hands raised in what I hoped passed for calm and not the universal sign for *please don't strangle me.* "You reacted in a stressful moment.

You're overwhelmed. Anyone would be after what you've been through. And anyone can snap and do things they regret." Except that most people don't end up committing manslaughter with a leash.

"I didn't want anyone to find out," she whispered. "Especially not my husband. He'd never forgive me."

"Your husband?" *Keep her talking. Try to talk her off the ledge. Maybe you can reach her rational side.*

She nodded miserably. "He thinks I'm fragile. I couldn't let him know I… snapped. I'm not a monster!" Her voice rose again, trembling.

A new survival instinct slammed into me.

Fragile people who insist they aren't monsters are *precisely* the ones who snap twice.

"Marilee," I said, soft as I could. "You need help. This is too big to carry alone. The police will take everything into consideration."

Her expression changed—subtle, but unmistakable. Something shuttered behind her eyes. Her shoulders straightened. Her breathing evened. She wasn't a sobbing mess anymore.

She was calculating.

"I *can't* let my husband know. He'll divorce me," she said, voice low and suddenly steady. She took a step closer.

I took a step back.

The mop bucket betrayed me again with a metallic wobble.

"You've always been kind to me," she said. "One

of the only ones. I don't want to hurt you."

My blood froze so hard I think it crystallized.

"Hurt me?" I repeated. My voice shot up an octave. Maybe two. "No one needs to hurt anyone! Let's just talk. Get everything sorted." Preferably with witnesses. I swallowed.

Merlin screamed again from the back room: "Help! Help! Bimbo! Bimbo!"

"Shut up!" she shouted past me, the first real flash of anger breaking through.

That was the moment I understood exactly how Margot's evening had gone.

"Okay," I said with a brittle nod, "I think we all need to calm down—"

"You're going to tell someone," she said. Not a question. A statement of fact. Her eyes sharpened. "I can't let that happen."

My stomach dropped to somewhere around my shoes. I took another step back, this time feeling for anything nearby I could use as a barrier—a broom, a mop handle, a conveniently placed tranquilizer gun, anything.

Nothing convenient presented itself. Why was there no mop in the bucket?

"Marilee," I whispered, my heart slamming so hard I felt it in my teeth, "you don't want to do this."

She reached for me.

Not fast. Not lunging. But with a deliberate, eerie calm.

That was somehow worse.

That was *so much worse*.

I backed up until my hips hit the reception counter so hard a stack of brochures avalanched to the floor. Marilee's beautifully manicured hands—complete with glittery nail art that said *Peace & Love* ironically—latched around my neck with shocking strength.

Survival instinct kicked in, and I hauled one knee upward to nail her in the abdomen. A whoosh of air escaped her lips along with an unladylike grunt, and her grip loosened.

In that split second of freedom, I did what any sensible person would have done five minutes earlier—turned and bolted toward the office like my life depended on it, because it apparently did. But, in my defense, terror had replaced every reasoning neuron in my brain before the fight or flight response finally decided to step in.

Marilee wasted no time in racing after me, slamming into my back and tackling me to the ground. We slid across the hardwood floor like two ice-skaters in a badly gone wrong routine. She landed on top of me. I was now at a distinct disadvantage, pinned under her body as she straddled me and wrapped her hands around my neck again.

"Help!" I croaked out, thrashing like a fish trying to shake off a heron. My fists shot out blindly, connecting with absolutely nothing except air. Regret shot through me. *Why* hadn't I armed myself with that scalpel?

She held on like a vice while simultaneously banging my head against the floor. My vision began to blur.

Then—fwump fwump fwump—the sound of wings. Merlin screeched, "Stupid bimbo!" at a decibel level that could shatter glass.

Mercifully, her hands disengaged from my throat, and she rolled off me, shrieking and flailing her arms, "Get it off of me!"

I fought to push myself upright, blotches of black patches still dancing before my eyes, stunned by the scene before me, which looked like a low-budget remake of *The Birds* with only one bird. Merlin dive-bombed like a feathery avenger sent from the heavens, his tiny chest puffed with righteous fury. I clutched my throat and sucked in long, ragged breaths.

Marilee tried ineffectively to rise while fending off the attack. "Get it away from me!" she yelled, swatting at Merlin.

After a long, paralyzing moment, I gathered what was left of my wits and leapt for the phone on the desk.

At the same time, I heard the back door open and a voice shouted, "Amanda! You in there?"

Kip. His footsteps pounded down the hall and into the room. He stopped dead in his tracks, taking in me— red-faced and wheezing, Marilee looking like she'd been mugged by a pigeon, and Merlin perched atop the filing cabinet, chest heaving like a prizefighter.

"What on earth is going on?"

Kip grabbed my arm, steadying me, and shot a look over my shoulder at Marilee. Her expression had twisted into something feral.

I tried to answer.

But all that came out was a strangled, gasping, utterly unhelpful, "Bimbo!—I mean—Merlin—Margot—leash—she killed her!"

Chapter Twenty-Six

Kip released me and converged on Marilee. "Stay where you are," he said, his tone suddenly all business, his body in pure police mode. "Don't move."

Marilee slumped into a chair, weeping and clutching her scratched face. Kip moved fast, snapping cuffs on her wrists before she could get her murderous mojo back. "Marilee Meece, you're under arrest for the murder of Margot Dilly, the attempted murder of Amanda Reynolds, obstruction of justice, and anything else I can think of. You have the right to remain silent . . ."

His words became buzzing in my ears. I gently cornered Merlin, scooped him up, and returned him to his cage.

"Good work, buddy," I said, leaving the cage in the surgery where he wouldn't have to see Marilee Meece again. He let out a wolf whistle.

Then I staggered out into the lobby and collapsed into a chair.

Kip marched Marilee out of the office and sat her down across from me. All the fight had gone out of her. She sat drained and pale, as if this whole situation were merely a bad dream. Either that, or her last functional brain cell had quietly retired.

"I've called for backup," he said. "We'll be taking her downtown and booking her." He reached over and took my hand. "Are you okay?"

I nodded. "I'm fine." Maybe that was stretching the truth just a little. I took a deep breath. "I just never suspected her. I didn't think I was in any danger when I met her here to take in a stray dog." Suddenly remembering the little dog, I said, "Speaking of which, where is she?"

Rising from the chair, my eyes scanned the room. There she was. Hiding under Marilee Meece's chair. The animal lover. The woman who couldn't stand injustice for animals but who had murdered a human being with her bare hands. And who had tried to kill me. I couldn't bring myself to go anywhere near her.

"Would you mind?" I inclined my head to Kip. He caught my line of sight and gallantly retrieved the trembling dog.

"I'll be right back," I said, as I disappeared into the kennel. Somehow, the mundane task of setting the stray up in a run with a bed, food, and water helped calm my nerves.

By the time I returned to the lobby, three police cars lit up the parking lot with enough flashing lights to illuminate the Las Vegas strip. Two officers ushered Marilee out, her shoulders drooped in defeat.

"I'll be right behind you," Kip told the officers. He turned back to me. "Are you sure you're okay?"

I sank back into my chair, my shaky legs giving way. "You know, if it weren't for Merlin, alerting me to the fact that she was the murderer, I would have simply taken in the dog, and Marilee and I would have left. I never would have suspected anything. Then again, if it weren't for Merlin, we might never have caught the murderer." I shuddered, thinking of how Merlin's big mouth had put me in a life-threatening situation, and then how he had valiantly fought to save me.

Kip deliberated my words for a moment as he ran his thumb over my hand, a gesture that sent tingles up my arm, although it seemed absurd to be tingling at a time like this unless from fright.

"I'm just glad you got here when you did." Then, the thought hit me. "By the way, why *are* you here?"

He let out a soft laugh. "You're not going to believe this. Stanley Quackenbush told us. He said he saw you and another woman sneaking into the back door of the shelter and worried you were up to something suspicious."

My head spun. So, my paranoia wasn't entirely off base. "Why was he driving past the shelter?"

Kip laughed again. "He was on his way to the

police station for questioning."

I shook my head. "I still don't understand why he would care if I was here. Unless he thought I was coming here to get the incriminating books."

"Too late for that. They are in police custody, and he is squirming in the hot seat as we speak. I don't think he's going to be able to wiggle out of this one."

"I suppose I have Stanley Quackenbush to thank for saving my life," I said grudgingly. After all, the worm still had a lawsuit hanging over my head.

"Well, if it makes you feel any better, technically, you have *me* to thank for saving your life." He grinned, which made my insides go mushy.

I grinned back. "If you really want to get technical, Merlin saved my life."

He chuckled. "Okay, if that's the way you want to see things, although it hurts my policeman's ego to be out-heroed by a bird." Then, his voice got all strange. "I don't know what I would have done if anything had happened to you."

It took a second for the words to register. Then my pulse hiccupped. "What do you mean?"

He blew out a short breath. "I mean, I really like you, Amanda. I have ever since the first day I met you. You were the only one here who didn't treat me like dirt, considering my cover story and all. You were kind and caring, and I could see your true heart for this place."

"What?" I sat up and stared at him. "Then why

did you practically laugh in my face when I accidentally blurted out I thought our coffee meeting was a date?"

He frowned. "I didn't laugh in your face."

"You did, too. You said, and I quote, 'You thought this was a date'?" And you smirked.

"You misunderstood. I was flattered. I didn't think you liked me. And, for the record, I didn't smirk. I smiled."

"What? You didn't think I liked you. Why?"

"That first night I asked you out, and you blew me off by making up some lame excuse about choir practice."

"For your information, that was the truth. I really did have choir practice. Besides, I thought you were a paroled felon." I punched his arm lightly.

He chuckled. "Oh, so you were holding my checkered past against me? What happened to 'judge not'?"

I crossed my arms over my chest. "Oh, please. You were holding my suspect in a murder case status against me."

"Amanda, I couldn't openly declare my feelings for you while this investigation was ongoing."

"No, but you didn't need to make me feel like a .. . like an interfering trouble maker, who was still under suspicion."

His gorgeous eyes twinkled. "I can't help it if the shoe fits."

I stuck out my lower lip in what I hoped was a pretty pout.

"Okay, how about if I try to make it up to you?"

I peeked up at him from beneath my lashes in shameless flirtation. "How?"

"Like this." He pulled me into his arms, then bent his head and pressed his lips against mine.

My head exploded in sensations I'd never known existed. Perhaps it was the adrenaline of the near-death experience. Or the fact that this whole nightmare was over. Maybe it was Kip declaring his feelings for me. Or perhaps it was the sweet release of my pent-up feelings for him. Whatever. It felt pretty darn good. And God certainly did move in mysterious ways.

Chapter Twenty-Seven

Of course, the arrest of Marilee Meece for the murder of Margot Dilly, as well as every chaotic event leading up to it, made headline news for all the local television channels and splashed across the front of the newspapers. Merlin and I became instant, although reluctant, celebrities, the kind who give awkward interviews and duck behind potted plants to avoid attention. Merlin also had trouble answering straightforward questions, but his natural charm endeared him to every reporter. Well, except for the lady from Channel Seven News, whom he called a stupid bimbo.

Vanessa and Tiffany, while grateful that I was alive, were nevertheless a little miffed that they had missed all the action. But at least they seemed to have bonded in their mutual resentment. Friendship, as well as God, works in mysterious ways.

Stanley Quackenbush, immensely relieved to be

off the suspect list for Margot's murder and staring down the indisputable ledgers naming him as Margot's partner in crime, finally admitted his involvement. Naturally, he twisted the truth into a pretzel, insisting he'd had no idea of Margot's criminal past when he hired her, and that he'd been duped by her "well-meaning but misguided bookkeeping."

He also, with astonishing dexterity, managed to pin the bulk of the blame on her. The county accepted his deal: he'd repay what Margot siphoned from the shelter and "voluntarily" step down as commissioner to "spend more time with his family." I'm sure Mrytle was positively overjoyed.

Then, in a final magnanimous act— performed for the cameras, no doubt—he dropped the lawsuits against Vanessa, Tiffany, and me. Although I would have liked to see him do jail time for his theft, rumor had it that the D.A. was leaning toward probation and community service. I just prayed he didn't plan to do his community service at the shelter.

The county appointed Gary as the permanent shelter director and reopened the shelter. Gary asked me to come back, and I agreed. I missed the furry chaos, not the felonious.

The following Sunday, I invited Kip to church to prove to him that I truly did sing in the choir and hadn't made up an excuse to avoid his invitation. When I entered the choir room to warm up, Yolanda swooped in on me like a hawk spying a field mouse.

"Amanda! What an awful ordeal. What was it like being alone with a killer?"

"Did you suspect Marilee Meece?" Kay chimed in, her eyes gleaming.

Within seconds, a small crowd surrounded me, all talking at once. Questions pinged at me like hailstones. I suddenly understood why celebrities wear sunglasses indoors.

Then, before I could formulate a single reply, a strong arm curled around my shoulders and pushed me through the mob with the efficiency of a seasoned linebacker. Leading me to a chair, Stella Ramsey's loud voice rose. "People! Amanda has been through enough. Let her have some breathing room." She stood protectively in front of me, daring anyone to breach the space around us.

Instant, sheepish silence ensued. Chagrined looks crossed several faces as they backed away like cats halfway up the curtains, pretending they meant to be there. Stella dropped into the chair next to me and stroked my hair with a tenderness that caught me off guard.

"We should offer up a prayer of thanks that the Good Lord rescued our dear Amanda out of the lions' den."

Then she bent her head and launched into a prayer. As I listened to her warm, earnest expression of thanks to the Good Lord, a sense of peace swirled over me, as well as a sense of shame for the way I'd secretly maligned her singing voice. Stella had a pure heart, a sweet spirit, and a way of making people feel they mattered. I could learn a lot from this woman.

We ran through the anthem, then filed out through the hallway and into the choir loft just as the organist was finishing "It is Well with My Soul." I couldn't have picked a more fitting hymn for the several days I'd survived. I looked out into the congregation and saw Tiffany, Vanessa, and Kip sitting in the fifth row. They gave me big smiles and a thumbs-up.

After the service, Tiffany and Vanessa headed to lunch—without me. That was okay because I preferred to be in Kip's company.

As he helped me into his car, he said, "Who was that woman sitting next to you in the choir loft? The one with the dreadful voice?"

I turned to him. "Stella? Your hearing must be off. I think she has the voice of an angel."

The look he gave me said he wasn't buying it.

I pulled into the shelter parking lot the next morning with a ridiculous amount of optimism for someone who had recently survived an attempted murder. The sun was shining, the birds chirping, and someone had already spilled kibble across the area leading to the dumpster. Business as usual. Gary met me inside with a grin that stretched nearly to his ears.

"Welcome back," he said, handing me a stack of intake folders as if I'd never left. "We're already behind. Perfect timing."

I flipped through the files. Vaccination records, surrender forms, the usual chaos—until a name jumped out at me.

My own, in Margot Dilly's handwriting.

Gary winced. "Yeah. We're still finding her, uh… creative paperwork. That one's from three weeks ago. Supposedly, 'you' examined a twelve-year-old Shih Tzu and wrote that it had the 'joints of a puppy and the constitution of a small warhorse.' The owner called me about it this morning."

I studied the record faxed from her veterinarian beneath Margot's form. "This dog is missing half its teeth."

"And, according to her veterinarian, she has arthritis in all four legs," he added. "But apparently Margot felt it needed a confidence boost."

I shook my head, laughing. "I swear, that woman had quite the imagination. She could sure write good fiction. I shudder to think of the things we'll unearth over the next few months."

We shelved the file. Gary peered into the carrier in my hand, holding the last kitten. She leapt toward the door, her crooked tail twitching.

"I don't think Marilee Meece is going to be able to take this one after all," I said, as I opened the door, scooping up the kitten. "I don't believe they allow pets in prison."

"Well, it looks like her husband's high-priced lawyer is trying to finagle a temporary insanity plea. But the good news is that Mr. Meece still wants to support the shelter because it meant so much to her."

Pleasantly surprised, I said, "Wow, that's really nice of him."

Gary shrugged. "And perhaps he feels some sense of guilt and responsibility for how his wife managed to embroil the shelter in a murder scandal."

The kitten burrowed under my chin with a squeaky purr far too big for her body. Over the past several days, I had grown quite fond of the kittens. "I'm afraid I'm going to be downgraded from Eleanor's favorite human."

As I cuddled the little tortie, I glanced around the shelter: the chorus of barking, the buzzing phones, and Merlin calling out, "Welcome to the Dalton County Animal Shelter," to someone who'd come through the front door. It felt good. It felt right. It felt like *my* chaos again.

And—for the first time in days—I felt entirely safe.

That evening, I curled up on the couch with Kip, the kitten asleep on my chest. He brushed a stray hair from my cheek. "So, this is the newest addition to your feline empire?"

"She's not part of an empire," I said primly. "I'm not officially a crazy cat lady with only two cats."

"Uh-huh." He rubbed the kitten's forehead. "Should I assume she'll be sleeping in your bed?"

"Absolutely."

"And Eleanor?"

"She doesn't get a vote."

Kip chuckled. "I'm glad this ordeal is over, and you're safe, Amanda."

"Me too," I said softly. "And who knows? With Margot's paperwork still surfacing, there may be more mysteries hiding around here than we realize."

He gave me a look somewhere between amused and worried. "Please tell me this is not foreshadowing."

I grinned and kissed him. "Oh, I have no doubt it is."

The kitten purred louder, as if agreeing.

And just like that, my life felt full again—cats, chaos, choir disasters, questionable commissioners, and all. With Kip beside me and a kitten on my lap, I was certain nothing else could possibly go wrong. I should really stop thinking things like that.

THANK YOU, DEAR READER

If you enjoyed reading this book, the best thing you can do to help the author is to tell others about it. Ellen would also greatly appreciate it if you could rate her book and leave a brief review on Amazon and Goodreads. Simply type in the name of the book and the author. When the website loads, click the book cover, then scroll down; you'll see a button to leave a rating and review. A review doesn't have to be long—a sentence or two telling what you liked about the book. Was it interesting, humorous, informative, thought-provoking, etc.? Thank you so much for your support.

Ellen would love for you to visit her website at https://ellenfannonauthor.com and subscribe to her weekly blog, *Good for a Laugh*.

Follow Ellen on Facebook: https://www.facebook.com/ellenfannonauthor.

Ellen Fannon is an award-winning author, a retired veterinarian, a former missionary, and a church pianist/organist. She and her retired Air Force pilot-turned-pastor husband have fostered more than forty children and have two adopted sons. Ellen has published eight novels, and her stories have appeared in *One Christian Voice, Chicken Soup for the Soul, Divine Moments, and Guideposts;* her devotions have appeared in *Open Windows, Guideposts God's Creatures, and The Secret Place.*

Please visit Ellen's website, *Good for a Laugh*, and sign up to follow her weekly blog at ellenfannonauthor.com

Hounded by Murder — Discussion Questions

1.   Amanda volunteers at the animal shelter for the right reasons, yet her good intentions land her in serious trouble. How does the theme of "no good deed goes unpunished" play out in the story?

2.   The new shelter director quickly becomes unpopular. At what point did you begin to suspect something more sinister beyond poor management? Were you surprised by the depth of her nefarious activities?

3.   Amanda becomes a police suspect largely because she finds the body. How does this suspicion affect her decisions and behavior throughout the investigation? Would you have acted differently in her place?

4.   Several characters have motives for wanting the director gone. Which suspect did you find most convincing—and why? Did your suspicions change as the story progressed?

5.   Humor is woven into moments of stress and danger throughout the book. Did the comedic elements enhance your enjoyment of the mystery or provide relief from the darker themes? Which scene made you laugh the most?

6.   Amanda's veterinarian background plays a meaningful role in the investigation. How does her profession give her unique insight? How does it complicate her involvement?   How does her professional background set her apart from other amateur sleuths you've read?

7.   The story highlights ethical issues surrounding animal welfare, shelter management, and accountability. What real-world parallels did you notice, and how did they affect your emotional investment in the story?

8.   Friendship and community play an important role as Amanda works to clear her name. Which supporting character added the most to the story, and why?

9.   Without spoilers, discuss the ending. Were you satisfied with the resolution? Did the clues feel fair in hindsight?

10. The animals provide comfort, comedy, and sometimes chaos. Did any particular animal steal the scene for you?

<u>SAVE THE DATE</u>

2022 Christian Indie Award Winner

What if you were given the chance to rekindle the flame with your first love? What happened to all those girls who were mean to you in school? Should Hannah Jensen take the chance of attending her high school reunion to find out?

Hannah hasn't been back to her hometown in twenty-five years. Now a widow raising a teenage daughter, she has the opportunity to go home for her twenty-fifth high school reunion. The invitation to the reunion stirs up a lot of old memories at the same time she is dealing with loneliness, the challenges of single-parenting a teenager, people who want to "set her up" with eligible men, her own insecurities, and her eccentric family.

The story interweaves the present with scenes from Hannah's past and her fantasy of "happily ever after" with her high school boyfriend in a humorous and entertaining manner. Her feelings from being "shunned" by the cool kids resurface as she reflects back on her time as a teenager. There are several roadblocks on Hannah's journey from a teenager through her present. The growing pains and amusing situations in which she finds herself are ones to which we all can relate. As she walks the path of self-discovery, she also discovers the most important life lesson of all–her relationship to God.

<u>**DON'T BITE THE DOCTOR**</u>

Real doctors treat more than one species. At least that's what veterinarian, Jill Bennet tells herself. On any given day, she may find herself doctoring dogs, cats, bunnies, birds, horses, pigs, or any other furry or feathered patient who crosses her path— striving daily to deliver compassion and competence to all God's creatures, in accordance with Colossians 3:23. Now, with over forty years of practice under her belt, Jill reflects back to her time as a new, young veterinarian in the early eighties—a time when women veterinarians were just beginning to become a presence among the previously male-dominated profession. Out in the real world, Jill finds herself in situations never covered in veterinary school. It is a journey of learning and laughter, as Jill contends with a variety of animal patients and their eclectic humans attached to the other end of the leash (and the checkbook), as well as less-than-helpful co-workers. Interwoven into this mix of new experiences is her budding romance with the owner of the sock-eating Labrador Retriever. *Don't Bite the Doctor* promises to bring smiles and tears to anyone who has ever been owned by an animal.

OTHER PEOPLE's CHILDREN

As a mid-thirties childless woman, Robin has all the answers on proper parenting. It doesn't take long, however, for Robin to realize that her perfect parenting ideas and reality often collide – the result being an amusing journey of finding out that God, indeed, has a sense of humor. As she deals with the baggage, idiosyncrasies, unique personalities, and special gifts of each child that crosses her path, she finds that there is no "one-size fits all" to parenting. However, in spite of the challenges she and her husband face, they are determined to become the children's strongest advocates in a flawed system that often fails the very victims it is designed to protect. The journey is often heartbreaking and frustrating, but these foster parents are firmly resolved that for whatever time they have children in their care, the children will know they are safe, protected, and loved by God, as well as by their foster parents.

<u>HONOR THY FATHER EPISODE ONE</u>

<u>HONOR THY FATHER EPISODE TWO</u>

Why should Adam's daughters, with whom he hasn't had contact for twenty-five years, honor him now when he needs a life-saving bone marrow transplant? Why should his son, who was kicked out of the house, honor his father? Is there any hope of reconciliation when twenty-five years of anger, bitterness, and divergent pathways have led family members down different roads of life? *Honor Thy Father* is the compelling story of loss and redemption and how God can turn tragedy into triumph.

How does a family survive after being torn apart? Adam Wallace copes with the heartbreaking loss of his wife and daughters by immersing himself in his work.

Charlotte withdraws from everyone and everything around her. Dana, living a life of privilege, does not even realize her loss. Katrina copes by trying to make everyone else happy. Scott copes by rebellion. Ultimately, they all come to realize that God can work through every situation to make beauty out of ashes.

<u>LOVE IN THE WIND</u>

<u>Book 1 in the Love in the Wind Series</u>

<u>2024 Living Water Award Winner</u>

Wyoming rancher Ben Parish is struggling to keep his ranch afloat. Veterinarian Darcy Fuller has moved to Wyoming to start a new life, but is struggling to become established in a new area. Both have been badly burned by past relationships and are not looking to become involved in another. When their paths cross, Darcy has an idea to bring extra income to the ranch, as well as provide her with an outlet for her passion for working with horses. But can their growing attraction coexist with a business partnership?

<u>FALLING FOR A COWBOY</u>

<u>Book 2 in the Love in the Wind Series</u>

Biology professor, Kendra Clark, is an independent, competent, intelligent woman of faith—that is, until she is around cowboy, Ricky Gaither. Then she becomes a babbling klutz. For his part, Ricky doesn't have much use for intellectuals or God. But when they keep running into each other, they can't deny their growing attraction. Can a relationship work between two people who seem to have nothing in common? Or does the secret Ricky harbors make them more alike than Kendra realizes? And will that secret derail any hope for a relationship?

LOVE'S TRAIL OF REDEMPTION

Book 3 in the Love in the Wind Series

Cam Ellis and Olivia Anderson have worked at Whispering Winds Ranch for two years without paying much attention to each other—until suddenly, things change. They are a perfect match in every way, except for the one challenge neither of them expected to enter their lives.

Will an event from Cam's past hold him hostage to moving forward, or can he overcome his deepest fear to risk everything for love?

DOGGED BY MURDER

Veterinarian Amy Dixon thought she was just helping out at the county dog show. Instead, she ends up in a dog-eat-dog world of rival breeders, pampered pooches, and one very dead Chihuahua breeder.

All Amy wanted was a quiet day filling in for a sick colleague. What she got was a snarling confrontation with Mildred Blankenship, the queen of the Chihuahua circuit—followed by a front-row seat to a growing list of people who'd be *just fine* if Mildred took her last lap around the show ring.

Then Mildred drops dead, and it turns out someone wasn't bluffing.

With Amy suddenly in the doghouse as a murder suspect, she teams up with charming snack-stand guy Nick Wyman to sniff out the real killer. But as they dig into the tangled leashes of show dog drama, they realize this mystery has more twists than a poodle's perm.

Will Amy and Nick find the culprit before someone else gets collared—or are they about to be the next ones put down?